echo

FRANCESCA LIA BLOCK

JOANNA COTLER BOOKS
An Imprint of HarperCollins*Publishers*

Echo

Copyright © 2001 by Francesca Lia Block

Printed in the United States of America. For information address
HarperCollins Publishers, 1350 Avenue of the Americas, New York, NY 10019.

www.harpercollins.com

Library of Congress Cataloging-in-Publication Data

Block, Francesca Lia.

Echo / by Francesca Lia Block.

p.   cm.

Summary: Jealous of her perfect mother and ignored by her artist father, Echo seeks
attention and healing from a variety of people living in beautiful Los Angeles.

ISBN 0-06-028127-8 — ISBN 0-06-028128-6 (lib. bdg.)

[1. Los Angeles (Calif.)—Fiction.] I. Title.

PZ7.B61945 Ec 2001   00-054234

[Fic]—dc21   CIP

                                                      AC

Typography by Alicia Mikles

1   2   3   4   5   6   7   8   9   10

❖

First Edition

DEC 06 2001 BWS

My Mother, The Angel

My father calls her The Angel. I am never sure how to live up to such a mother. She is almost six feet tall. The planes of her face are like carved ivory. The long neck and smooth eyelids and high cheekbones of Nefertiti's famous bust. Strawberry hair cascading to her hips like Botticelli's Venus. Pretty impossible to compete with when you are just under five feet with faded brown hair and the face of an elf.

My mother can make flowers bloom

with the slightest touch of her hand. Her garden burgeons—irises glitter as if embedded with silver, roses turn colors no one can match. Rose breeders come to find out her secrets but she only smiles mysteriously. They try to analyze the clippings she gives them but it is useless—the magic ingredient is her touch. Her birds of paradise are almost as tall as she is, her ranunculus look like peonies, her fruit trees bear lemons that taste like oranges and oranges the size of grapefruits. She can grow star-gazer lilies whose pollen is as thick soft hot pink powdered as expensive blush, and abundant peonies that people say only bloom in cooler climates. No jasmine ever smelled so sweet, bathing the insides of my nostrils and mouth with its twinkling white-and-lavender fragrance.

My mother wanders around the garden in the hills of Hollywood putting her ear to the cup of the petals or to the ground and, smiling mysteriously, proceeds to trim or water or fertilize each plant according to its own personal instructions. Sometimes I wake in the night and I swear I can hear the flowers in the garden singing my mother's name through the open window.

These things prove that my mother is not of this world. Don't they?

If there is any doubt, it would be quelled by contact with my mother's healing powers. When my father or I have any kind of cold, headache or muscular pain, she touches us in such a way that the discomfort vanishes. A strange breath of rose and mint fills the room and then everything is better.

Unfortunately for me, my mother's healing powers do not extend to transforming a plain girl into a girl so beautiful that it would not have surprised anyone to learn that this girl's mother was a celestial being. She does not have potions to make one's limbs long and one's skin glow. She doesn't believe in coloring your hair or wearing makeup. Why should she? Her eyes seem naturally kohl-lined. Her hair naturally hennaed. She is not particularly into fashion. She only needs a few gauzy dresses that she makes herself and some bare Grecian sandals that lace up her long amber legs. High-priced fashion would be a waste on her; it would be extraneous. Therefore, she rarely took me shopping when I was growing up. She told me I was beautiful without lip gloss or mascara. But, then, angels see beneath the surface of things.

How else is my mother like one?

"Her cooking!" my father says. "Her cooking is the cooking of a seraphim!"

She makes tamale pies, spinach lasagnas, Indian saffron curries, coconut and mint Thai noodles, grilled salmon tacos with mango salsa, persimmon bread puddings and lemon-raspberry pies, each one in minutes and without ever glancing at a recipe. She can never duplicate a dish twice since she doesn't write anything down and is always too excited about what she will make next, so my father and I are sometimes left pining for a reenactment of the almond enchiladas or the garlic-tomato tart. But we always have something else to look forward to. And my mother's food has almost narcotic effects—no matter how depressed or agitated we feel before dinner, we always relax afterwards into a dreamy stupor.

Also, my mother never gets angry. No matter what happens she always has a placid smile on her glowing Egyptian-artifact face. Sometimes I secretly wish that she would lose her temper and perhaps I even taunt her a little, to test her, but nothing works. My mother is unruffleable. She is like the da Vinci Madonna with a crescent moon hung on her mouth.

How wonderful, everyone thinks, to have a mother who is an angel, who never loses her temper, who can make birthday cakes even when it isn't your birthday— cakes so delectable as to be almost hallucinogenic—a mother who can take away the itch of insect bites with a whisk of cool fingers over your skin. People envy me my mother. A few children, encouraged by their parents, tried to befriend me just so they could come over and get clippings from my mother's garden and leftovers from her refrigerator. But no one realizes the difficulties of having an angel for a mother. It can make you feel rather insignificant, especially when boys ask you out just so they can catch a glimpse of her, waving good-bye, braless and in gauze, from the front porch. Especially when your father forgets to pick you up from school because he is out buying new lingerie for her again (even though she will forget to wear it) or when you ask him a question at dinner about your homework and he takes fifteen minutes to answer because he is gazing into the illuminated peony of her face.

My father found religion when he found my mother. He made the house a shrine, decorated with larger-than-life-size paintings and carvings of her. He lit candles and incense and sat and meditated every day. Unlike his mother, who died when he was eleven, my mother, who is years younger than he is, represents the nubile and healthy goddess who would never break his heart by leaving before he did. In this way she is eternal. She is his unprecedented blossom, his chocolate-cherry-swirl birthday cake, ultimately his angel.

I try to be grateful for my mother's graces and the love between my parents. It is a much better situation than most of what I have seen around me. Perhaps if I looked a little like my mother it wouldn't bother me at all. But as it is, I drift through her almost obscenely perennially lush garden, through her sacred kitchen, past the altar with the many images of her flickering in candlelight day and night, and wonder why just a little of the magic in the house could not settle on the bones and skin of my face or manifest through the tasks of my hands.

I am not angelic in the least. I smoke cigarettes and drink beer (my mother, after a brief stint with sugar in her youth, is utterly pure in terms of what she consumes). I can't cook or garden. I scald soups and plants die under my care. I have been known to fly into rages, especially before my period and especially if The Angel happens to placidly remind me that it is before my period. Occasionally, and mostly under premenstrual duress, I have stolen things—underwear, nail polish and lip gloss. The only things I know how to do well are shoplift, kiss and dance. None are particularly saintly virtues. And when I say dance, I'm not talking about ballet. My dancing is wild and unruly. I failed miserably at ballet although my mother had, of course, been coveted by the New York City Ballet when she was a child but had decided that she could not leave her family at that time because they needed her cooking and gardening and healing skills more than she needed the fame and fortune of the dance.

But ever since I was a little girl I captured neighborhood boys and made them sit in the basement and watch me. I dressed up in silk scarves and stolen

underwear and played songs whose beat I
could feel deep between my legs. While
I danced a strange thing occured. I would
have visions of what had happened to the
boys. I saw boys being beaten, boys being
shamed, boys crying, boys beating so they
wouldn't cry. Sometimes the visions made
me cry, too. When the dance was over I
would kiss the boys. We rolled around the
dusty musty basement floor in a tangle of
sweat and music. I loved how they smelled
and the taut smooth warmth of their
bodies. They moaned with pleasure and
whispered my name. Then they left and
never came back. Although some of them
would eye me with a mixture of longing
and anxiety at school. My dancing would
never have gotten me noticed by the New
York City Ballet. But I did know how to

move my hips, fondle my breasts, lick my lips, kick my legs, run my hands along my inner thighs, fall into the splits, writhe on the floor and remove wisps and slips of clothing while tears of passion slid down my face, so hot that it felt as if they were burning paths into my cheeks.

I wonder, is my mother angelic because she loves my father so much or does my father love my mother so much because she was always an angel? Was she born that way or was her angelic nature intensified by meeting him? Either way I'm not sure what that means as far as I am concerned, in terms of ever finding anyone who would love me as much as my father loves my mother, or whom I could love the way she loves him.

My mother told me once that I was a

miracle. Doctors said my father couldn't have children but my mother never gave up. And then she had me. Am I the miracle? Or is she?

When I was little, and still really just an appendage of my mother, my father expressed his love to me as if I really were one of her limbs. He carried me around like a good-luck charm, showing me off to the people who came to the gallery on La Cienega to buy his paintings.

"The little angel," he called me.

If I cried my father was usually the first one to take me in his arms and comfort me. He felt like soft caramel-colored corduroy and smelled like the cigarettes everyone smoked at his art openings and in the teachers' lounge, and like turpentine. He called me darling so frequently that I hardly

knew I had another name and sometimes
forgot when I had to answer to it at school.
When I was big enough to hold a pencil he
sat and drew with me. He put my drawings
up all over the house, right beside his paintings. He even let me put paint on his
canvases. He brought me with him to the
art classes he taught at the university and
gave me my own easel and paper and charcoal sticks. Then he gave me watercolors,
acrylic paints and finally oils. I felt drunk
on the smell of turpentine, the mystery of
mixing colors on the palette. When I
painted I felt proud and beautiful. I felt like
my mother's daughter.

My father painted me almost as much
as he painted my mother then. He painted
me as a baby nursing at her breast, sleeping on her belly, peeking out from her

backpack. As I got older he painted me sketching or reading with her. When I looked at the paintings later, I did not recognize myself. I looked just like a tiny version of my mother, her third breast, her second head, her miniature twin. At first I thought that I had changed a lot growing up, but when I saw photographs of myself—a little pale and pointed face, eyes always worried, peeking out from behind my mother's swirling gauzy body— I realized that this was not the case; my father was just painting me the way he wanted me to be.

As I grew older my father painted me less and less. By the time I had breasts I had disappeared from his canvases altogether. For a while I could come into his studio dressed in exotic getups and I would dance for him, trying to see who he was. All I saw were visions of my father falling in love with my mother. Sometimes I came bearing my latest painting of a wild Beauty with a body made of lurid open flowers, hoping to get his attention, but he ignored me and my work. He even painted a piece called "Family Portrait" which depicted my mother—in her flower garden.

Before that summer these were the worst of my problems—an angel mother, a distracted and sometimes neglectful father. Then everything changed. Just when I needed my mother's powers most, they seemed to be failing. The doctors told my father he was dying.

My mother would not believe it. She began to cook.

She concocted potions full of odd Chinese roots. The burdock was long and black and hairy, the lotus roots were like pinwheels or flowers. The food of the immortals, my mother said. She soaked the seaweeds called wakame and kombu. She peeled the thin beige skins off gnarled hunks of ginger. She made brown rice and tofu and miso soup from a golden paste.

The house had to be assessed. My mother went around throwing out all the chemicals that might have toxic properties and putting crystals everywhere—in teacups and cereal bowls, in the bathtub, all over the windowsills and altars. First, she soaked the crystals in salt water in the sun to purify them. The house was a mess of rainbows. Rainbows poured across the walls. The crystals reminded me of tiny

cities with cathedrals and towers. Sometimes I took the smaller ones and sucked
on them like rock candy but they had a
slightly bitter flavor. Then, guilty, I put
them in a glass of salt water on the win-
dowsill to make them pure again.

My mother bought books about healing and taught herself acupressure and
massage. She bought a massage table and
set it up in the bedroom. Delicate watery
music spilled through the house. The
rooms smelled of lavender and aloe and
eucalyptus.

She wanted to heal him all by herself,
with her roots and her hands and the songs
I heard her singing to him at night, lulla-
bies like the ones she once sang to me,
filling up the house like rainbows from the
crystals. But after a while my mother real-

ized that it wasn't going to be enough. She drove him to the hospital for the treatments even though I know she hated them. She just washed her hair so it shone and put on a fresh dress and drove him there and sat with him and tried to smile at the doctors, who were entranced and, she hoped, inspired, by her beauty, and then she brought him home to her soups and her songs and her flowers. She made him a silk beret to hide his naked head. She cooked up strange-smelling herbs and gave him the tea to drink.

While my mother did these things all I could manage to do was go to clubs, get drunk, smoke cigarettes and sleep. In the burning heat of that summer, even after the sun went down, it hardly cooled. I wore the night like one of the vintage dresses I collected from thrift stores—a purple silk with rhinestone star buttons. The crickets shrieked.

I went to a nightclub in a Greek restaurant on the east end of Melrose with plaster reproductions of classical statues standing around the dance floor. There was something creepy about the flat white spaces of their eyes, I thought. I bought a rum and Coke with my fake i.d. and drank it quickly (always thirsty) until my own eyes felt like Christmas lights. My dance partners were David and Venus de Milo. Although he was not the most captivating conversationalist or dynamic dancer, he was pleasing to look at. She was missing many body parts but also quite lovely. At least I could pretend I had companions.

I came home and went to bed realizing

how long it had been since I had been touched by anyone. I sucked my arms to help myself fall asleep. The next day I had to hide the bruises.

My mother was so busy caring for my father that she didn't notice when I stopped eating. Even though I was ravenous all the time I controlled my appetite most of the day. Then, late at night, after a few drinks, when the clubs closed, I went to all-night fast-food stands and ate burritos in my car in big gulps, squishing the beans and cheese out of the flour tortilla. My car smelled like grease that summer, and the steering wheel shone from my handprints. The next morning, disgusted, I wiped and aired out my car and vowed not to eat all day. This lasted until about two A.M. Sometimes instead of burritos I ate powdered sugar donuts with colored sprinkles. The powdered sugar cut and stung my mouth. The sprinkles reminded me of the lights of the city, shiny and sugary and fake and promising and nothing. That summer tasted like a powdered sugar donut stinging my mouth.

I decided to make my hair a different color so I went to see Mars at his West Hollywood salon. Mars called himself that because he was obsessed with space; he was determined to find evidence of aliens. While he trimmed my hair, Mars rhapsodized about his journeys out to the desert. He discovered secret government testing sites where there was evidence of alien landings. These areas were completely off limits to the public but Mars managed to sneak under fences and across

barricades with his camera. He showed me
a series of blurry photographs of marks on
the sand. His eyes flashed like spaceships
and his mouth salivated when he spoke.
I worried that he would cut my bangs
unevenly.

This time it was much worse than that.
Mars was showing me a circular burn mark
on his forearm. He said it was some kind
of secret government tactic to keep him
from visiting the alien sites. He was so
excited about the mark, which he believed
was more pure evidence to prove his the-
ory, that he didn't concentrate on my hair.
I should have come back another day but I
was determined. I told Mars I wanted to
look glamorous. What I really meant was,
I wanted to look so beautiful that I could
forget that my father was sick, beautiful

enough that a boy would love me the way my father loved my mother, beautiful enough that when my parents looked at me they would forget their pain. I knew Mars couldn't do that but I thought he might be able to help a little.

Mars stopped ogling his burn mark, ran his fingers through his gold metallic hair, shook his head so that his many gold hoop earrings jangled and said, "I have just the thing." I was imagining shades of Marilyn and Jean Harlow to make me glow in the dark, but when Mars rinsed my hair I saw that it was not platinum at all but a frightening ghoulish shade of light green.

Did he mean to make me into a Martian? Mars insisted it was a mistake, that he had intended something else, but

that he thought it looked fabulous, and,
besides, if we tried to dye over it or bleach
it out my hair might all break off, and
maybe it was some kind of sign the aliens
were projecting to him through me, to not
give up and keep searching for them.

I was unable to speak. Mars didn't
charge me and I left trying to force the
tears back down my throat. My mother
could have carried off the green hair. She
would have looked like a sea goddess. But
I was elfin and small and now, clownish.
And ashamed, too, that something like this
would make me cry.

Instead of going to a club I just drove.
I drove the freeway past medieval castles
and neon crosses and raggedy palm trees.
I drove under bridges and past walls decorated with murals of runners, cops, movie

stars, Betty Boop and one old lady with
crystal-ball blue eyes and a crocheted quilt.
When it was late enough they seemed alive,
staring at me with their eyes and reach-
ing out for me with their hands. I liked to
drive fast to feel as if I was getting away.
I played music as loud as possible and
screamed the lyrics until my throat was
sore.

When I got home, late, I crept into
the kitchen to get something to eat. My
mother was lying on the kitchen table,
naked. Moonlight shone through the window illuminating her body and the crystals
she had placed all over herself. She looked
like a crystal statue from a tomb.

I stepped behind the door. After a while
my mother removed the crystals from her
breasts and abdomen, stood up and walked

to her bedroom. I followed her and pressed my ear to the door.

I heard my mother say to my father, "Give it to me."

"What?" asked my father. He sounded as if he were talking in his sleep. "What, darling?"

"Give me the disease."

"No," he said. "No, I can't do that."

"I know what to do with it," she said. "I'm stronger than ever."

"No! I would never let you have it!" my father said. He was fully awake now.

"I would rather die than live without you," my mother whispered.

I had known my father felt this way. But not my mother. My mother who had never once seemed afraid.

In their bedroom it was silent.

The next night I went out again. To a dank beery underground club near Hollywood Boulevard, filled with vampiric-looking boys and girls, some of whom wore tiny red-stained pointed caps on their incisors; at least I assumed they were caps. They drank the blackest red wine and crammed together in booths admiring their veins. There was one boy who had two lumps on his scalp; he was proudly showing them off to two girls and insisting they were horns. They looked more like the result of too much head banging to me. The boy jumped onstage and started to yell into the microphone about cancer. He looked right at me and his eyes and mouth shone like a jack-o'-lantern. He pointed his finger at me until I left.

I drove to the ocean. I liked to try to notice the exact moment when the air changed and I could smell the sea. Sometimes the smog was too much and I couldn't taste salt on my lips until I was almost right there. But this night was late enough and I got the smell way before. The ocean seemed to be calling me. I turned off the music and listened for it whispering. Maybe I would become a mermaid. I had the right hair. I would live in the swirling blue-green currents, doing exotic underwater dances for the fish, kissed by sea anemones, caressed by seaweed shawls. I would have a dolphin as a friend. He would have merry eyes and the thick sleeked flesh of a god. My fingernails would be tiny shells and my skin would be like jade with light shining through it. I

would never have to come back up or go
to clubs again. Boys would never send me
away untouched and empty. I would never
need cigarettes or vodka. It wouldn't matter that my mother could not keep my
father from dying. Nothing would matter.

I was drinking a six-pack of beer, sitting on the sand at my favorite beach, a
little private cove with black pebble sand
where almost no one came even in the day,
and I noticed a tiny light in lifeguard stand
#9. It was a deserted stand that had been
boarded up, with a big sign: NO LIFE-
GUARD ON DUTY. SWIM AT YOUR OWN
RISK. But the light was unmistakable. And
eerie in the misty darkness, like a dropped
star, a scudding flame. Then I saw someone sitting at the top of the stand. It was
a skinny boy with lots of dark curly hair.

That was all I could tell. He was slouched over, his elbows on his bent knees, and he was looking out at the dark, moon-iced, foam-sizzled waves intently, as if he could see whales or dolphins or magic islands or phantom ships.

Then I wanted to go into that water. I wanted it so badly that my mouth stung like salt and my skin tingled and I stood up and ran down to the shore. I wanted to go into the waves and find the thing the boy saw. I knew that it was better than what I was, than what my life was. It was something deep and far and soothing and dark and bright. It was without pain. It was like falling into the surging liquid herd of waves and becoming one of them and becoming nothing and everything at once.

I was a mermaid. I had green hair. I

could go deeper and farther.

But I'd had too many beers. The water was so cold. And the waves were stronger than they seemed. Right away I knew it was too much. Part of me reached up like a hand trying to grasp for air but part of me sank in so easily like a fist, plunging deep deep in, flooded with sea until it was inside of me—a lover, in my lungs and in my heart and I was no longer the daughter of a dying man and an angel who could not save him but the daughter of the water.

The part of me that was the hand, though, it must have reached up. It must have seen the foam of the stars and the waves of the night sky and wanted that, too, and somehow now, the boy on the beach is running he is running toward me, having seen, not dolphins or whales or islands or treasure ships, but a drowning green-haired girl who may or may not want to be rescued but he will swim to her and he will buoy her up in his arms and he will drag her to shore where her head is writhing with seaweed and her eyes are pummeled stones and in the black sea that follows, he will be her breath.

In the hospital I asked them how I got there and they told me a young man had brought me and then left. I knew who he was and I knew where I could find him.

I had decided not to tell my parents what had happened to me. Besides, what could they have done? They had other things to worry about; they'd hardly noticed that I'd been gone all night. I was fine, I told myself. I told myself I was lucky.

After a few days I went back to the beach to find the boy who had saved me. I saw the little candle burning in the lifeguard stand and I saw him sitting in the exact same position as the other night, staring out at the water. I stood looking up at him and he nodded his head, very slightly, but he didn't move. His curly hair was all in his face and he had on a pair of big funny glasses that had broken and been taped together and he was wearing a baggy T-shirt and faded shorts and he was barefoot.

"Thank you," I said.

He nodded again.

I told him my name was Echo.

And that was how I met him. My silent friend. My lifeguardian. The boy with the secrets on his back, the boy who never said what he was called.

I went to see him every night. We built
sand castles with arches and columns and
moats and turrets and hidden passageways.
I hated to lose the castles, but he nodded
and seemed to say, *This is a part of it,*
watching them demolished by the waves.
We would sit for hours watching the waves
break against the shore. Although he was
silent I knew what he was thinking, about
how he had dreamed of the singing and
flashing and how it had seemed so far away
and now here he was beside it on a night
so warm we could have been naked, bask-
ing in moon. Sometimes he played me
melodies on his battered mandolin or his
old accordion. The music was sweet and
sad like rain and trains and leaves in wind.
I just liked to sit near him, watching his
hair flop in his face as he strummed or

squeezed. I liked to sit close enough that
I could smell him. He smelled of sea and
salt and blueberries. I wondered if he
tasted that way. My mouth tasted of blueberries when I was with him. How did he
taste?

He must have kissed me that one time,
in his way, to save my life. But then he
never touched me again.

At home I watched my mother sitting at
my father's bedside, eternally radiant like a
candle that had hypnotized him with its
light. I wanted to be an angel for the boy
on the beach.

I wore white gauzy clothes and spoke
softly. I attempted to make sweet green
corn tamales but they hardened and stuck
to the corn husk so I brought him cheese
and apples instead. I did not bring him

flowers from my mother's garden—afraid
he would want to know who grew such
creatures—but I picked armfuls of wildflowers. I didn't smoke or drink in his
presence. If I felt upset I kept it to myself.
I didn't reveal anything about my mother,
my father or my past of lonely kissing
and desperate striptease. I thought these
things would send him running like the
boys who had appeared so mesmerized in
the basement but ignored me in the school
cafeteria.

My approach seemed to be working.
He wrote songs for me on the mandolin
and accordion; he built me palaces and at
dawn, when I left, his eyes shone like the
sun-sea-glimmered sand. But still he never
touched me.

My longing was starting to ache so

much I could hardly walk. I slept late and
staggered around the house. I was always
hungry but food didn't fill me so I mostly
stopped eating. I was more and more
thirsty the more I drank.

I wanted him. I felt it like an ocean filling every orifice, like the night I almost
drowned. I wondered if I were my mother,
if then he would touch me.

Sometimes I told myself I would have to
stop seeing him. I was going away to school
anyway, soon. I would find another boy
there, one who wanted me. But every time
I heard his music or saw his face or smelled
his saltberry scent I knew that I could
never stop wanting him. No matter how far
away I went or who I met. Who was he?

I asked one night as we sat on the shore
by our ruined sea castle watching the waves

break under the foam-white moon. He looked at me with so much sadness that I wished I hadn't said it.

It was not until two nights before I moved away that he told me.

There were so many tears inside of me but I was holding them in and he was sitting staring at the ocean through the lenses of his big strange glasses and I could feel his tenderness as if I were in his arms. But I wasn't in his arms.

"My father is dying," I said.

He looked at me. I saw his eyes shining behind his glasses. *This is a part of it*, he was saying. *But I wish it wasn't. I wish I could make it not.*

"My mother is perfect," I said. "I've always wanted to be like her. But I'm not. I've always been jealous of her. But now

I'm afraid all the things I'm jealous of are going to die when he does.

"I need you to touch me," I said.

He looked down at his hands. His whole body was shrouded in sadness. *I'm sorry*, he was saying.

"Who are you?" I asked. I was trying not to sob. I knew I would be leaving him so it really didn't matter but somehow I didn't want him to see me cry.

"Have I imagined you?" I asked. "If I'm imagining you then why can't I imagine you making love to me?"

He bent his head and pulled off his T-shirt. His body was lithe and brown, his shoulders slightly hunched. He turned his back to me and I saw what was hidden there, pressed damp and matted against his shoulder blades. The shabby soiled once-white feathers hung limply.

Then he huddled back down in the sand, hiding his back against the lifeguard stand.

Another angel. A real one. An angel for a love. An angel who wouldn't touch me. What was I supposed to do? With my wildness. With my rages. With my desire and my tears.

I left him that night. When I got home the fragrance of the flowers almost suffocated me. My mother had filled the house—they stood in vases and floated in bowls. My mother was wearing a wreath of roses. She was massaging my father's feet with eucalyptus oil. He had the look of an opium eater—his jaw slack, his eyes feverish.

I went into my room and locked the

door and blasted the music and got in bed and rubbed between my legs thinking of the boy on the beach. It went on and on until I was dry and sore. When I came it was in sobs.

The next night I went back to the sea dressed in 1950s silk travel scarves—Paris with the Eiffel tower and ladies in hats and pink poodles, Venice with bronze horses and gondoliers, New York in celestial blue and silver. I brought candles and lit the candles, all the candles, in a circle around the lifeguard stand and put a tape in my boom box. I came down that ramp with the sea lapping at my feet and the air like a scarf of warm silk and the stars like my tiara. And my angel was sitting there solemnly in the sand, sitting cross-legged like a buddha, with sand freckling his brown limbs and he watched me the way no boy had ever watched me before, with so much tenderness and also a tremendous sorrow, which was what my dances were about just as much, the sorrow of not being loved the way my womb, rocking emptily inside of me, insisted I be loved, the sorrow of never finding the thing I had been searching for.

What was the sorrow of this boy? As I danced the visions came. A boy crying under a bed in a dark room. A boy shivering from cold, dreaming of sun to burn the chill away. A wound on the inside of his thigh. A boy on a bus running away from home to live in a lifeguard stand by the sea, a boy who had pasted wings to his back as the only way he could escape the pain of who he had been before. A boy who could not touch because if he touched he

would remember things he needed to forget, reopen wounds he needed to keep
sealed. A boy who could be safe and
untouched as long as he was an angel, an
angel and not a boy.

Afterwards I came and lay beside him.
My heart was like the waves.

He took off his glasses and I saw,
clearly, for the first time, the bones of his
face. "Your heart is beating so hard," he
said into my hair.

His voice didn't startle me. It was as
if I'd heard it all those other times he'd
spoken silently.

"I was so scared," I said. "I was
shaking."

"You are beautiful, Echo."

Then I said, "It doesn't matter if we
never make love." I just needed him to see

me, feel what I felt. I just needed to dance
for him and lie like this by the sea, with our
tiny blue ark for when the flood came.

And then I cried a flood of tears as
if I really were a mermaid who had ab-
sorbed too much sea into herself. The
tears spilled like a balm, like a potion, like
a charm. In them swam a little girl whose
father was dying without ever having seen
her. In them swam a girl whose mother's
magic—the thing the girl envied more
than anything else in the world, the thing
that had made her invisible, the most pre-
cious thing—might be dying too. In them
swam a green-haired girl who had never
been touched by the boy to whom she was
so devoted that she would have lived with
him forever in a shack by the sea or a
ruined sand castle even if he never made

love to her. My tears were for me, but they were also for him. They were to wash away the thing that had frightened him so much so long ago. The thing that had hurt him so deeply. The wound inside his thigh. My tears poured out of me and he drank them down his throat. He drank them in gulps deep into himself, swallowing sorrow.

"Someday," he said, "when we are ready, I will give you back your tears."

When I looked up he was gone. I thought of the wings. Were they false were they real? They were beating inside of me.

Enchanted Hotel

Eva spent her days in the woods with her father, Sy, picking berries that ripened at the sight of her, swimming in lakes where fish and birds gathered to watch her, and studying the patterns of the wings of the butterflies that chased her. Meanwhile, her mother, Bella, stayed in the white wood-frame house overgrown with roses, writing stories. Then Bella was offered a job in the studios so she and Sy brought Eva to Hollywood.

Now Bella sat in a tiny bungalow on a movie lot, writing scripts that were stolen by producers who attached their starlet-girlfriends' names to them. Sy attempted to sell homes in the style of pagodas, castles, villas and chalets to people who never seemed to buy them. And Eva was left to fend for herself.

The jade-green hotel where they lived looked like a fairy-tale palace. Eva sat by the pool talking to the palm trees. She told them stories of eastern trees that changed colors and lost leaves, and heard palm tales of kissing movie stars and drowning children. Eva believed the place was enchanted, not realizing that she was the enchantment. She picked oranges and avocados when she was hungry and she floated in the water all day until her ivory skin turned to gold and

her hair grew even longer, down to her
knees, and people staying at the hotel
would stop speaking or choke on their
drinks when they saw her floating or
perched in a fruit tree with hibiscus flowers in her hair and powder-blue or pale-
yellow parakeets on her shoulders. A
famous movie director spotted her weaving
a nest out of twigs, branches, feathers and
dried flowers; she planned to put it up in a
tree so she could sleep closer to the moon
on the warm nights when the pool glowed
like a blue ghost. He was sure she was
some kind of supernatural being and that
if he could capture her on film he would
change the history of cinema. However, she
wasn't interested in becoming a film star,
afraid that it would take her away from her
family and corrupt her healing powers, so

she pretended to be deaf and mute whenever he was around. Eventually he gave up
and she was left alone to swim, build her
nest and care for her parents. She learned
to cook at that time, experimenting first
with mud-and-jacaranda blossom stew for
her bisque dolls who ate it voraciously and
began to develop an uncanny human glow
in their blue glass eyes, and eventually
gathering recipes and tips from the people
at the hotel. An Indian businessman taught
her about curries, the aphrodisiac properties of certain spices and how to make a
mango-yogurt concoction that was refresh-
ing on the most burning days when the
palm trees seemed about ready to ignite
from the Santa Ana winds sizzling through
their fronds. A couple who had come from
China to open a restaurant, familiarized her

with dishes employing mysterious healing roots. And a handsome Italian with fistfuls of black curls, dangerous cheekbones and hopes of becoming a matinee idol gave her his mother's secret recipe for risotto that shone in the dark. At the hotel Eva also learned secrets of a southern Californian garden from the three-foot-tall gardener who had played a munchkin in *The Wizard of Oz* and who knew how to breed impossibly green and silver hydrangeas, about the poisonous and thoroughly Los Angelean beauty of belladonna and oleander, and the arias that roses most enjoyed hearing. The plants immediately took to Eva and the garden at the hotel began to grow so profusely that the head gardener had to hire three more men to keep it from overgrowing the building. In the same way, all the exotic pet

birds from the houses in the hills flew away
from home to live nearer to the little girl.
The trees shook and flashed with them.
Stray dogs and cats also became a problem.
A silvery-taupe weimaraner with pale green
human eyes and a limp; an emaciated, low-
slung basset hound who tripped on his ears;
a blind honey-blond retriever with a perpetual grin; and various assorted mongrels
descended on the hotel, following Eva
around in a procession, bringing her flowering branches and offering her rides on
their backs. Cats came, too. They lolled at
the foot of the trees where she slept,
crawled in through her window and ate at
her table when her parents were out. The
dogs and cats grew fat, huge and glossy in
Eva's presence and from her care. She
groomed them, stroked them, played with

them and made them a special diet of turkey, oats and fresh vegetables. The blind retriever regained sight in one eye and the weimaraner stopped limping. They were so beautiful and good-natured under her influence that everyone at the hotel began to gladly welcome them into their own rooms and many canine and feline lives were saved.

One day, sitting at the soda fountain in the hotel cafeteria, Eva saw a man with shining sunken eyes and beautiful hands watching her over his cup of coffee and sketching strange sad-eyed creatures on his napkin. He was much older than she and never spoke to her, but she knew that he was in love with her and that one day they would meet again and become as inseparable as identical twins who looked nothing alike and had been born many years apart.

Sol was tall and thin and wore tiny round spectacles and a threadbare dark suit. Rose was very small, with a broad pale face. They met at a German synagogue when they were teenagers and never looked at anyone else again. After they married, Sol and Rose lived in a stone building full of candles and books, with window boxes of herbs and tiny vegetables. Sol taught philosophy to boys in a poorly lit basement. Rose was a milliner. She made hats piled with doves, flowers, cherries, peacock feathers, cupids for the rich women of the city. They were said to have certain unusual properties, the hats—love spells, fertility charms, talismans of prosperity and protection. But they were not magical enough.

When he was eleven, Sol and Rose's boy was sent away from his home to live with his aunt and uncle in New York. Before he left, Rose gave him her wedding dress wrapped in pale blue tissue and a box of paints and told him that if he ever wanted to communicate with her he could do so through his art. The boy had not understood what this meant. When he learned what happened to his parents, he became a little old man. He began to walk stooped over and the grief tasted like ash in his mouth. When he tried to paint images of the exotic birds and fruits that his mother loved, he ended up with monsters howling in dark storms and ripping their own limbs from their sockets.

So the boy began a desperate search for a woman with flowers growing out of her head, birds on her shoulders and the ability to mend broken hearts with her creations. There was no sign of her for years. Then he realized that he wouldn't find her in Manhattan, a city of dark stone and soot and noise and burning cold winters where nature had to be imported and relegated to certain areas like a caged animal. He imagined she was living in a sun-blossomed paradise, a city of magicians, movie queens, love-struck clowns. So he took the empty box of paints his mother had given him and the wedding dress wrapped in pale blue tissue paper and left the brownstone apartment, where he lived in a perpetual silence with his aunt and uncle, and went to Los Angeles to find her. Sitting at a soda

fountain in a hotel restaurant, he was
shocked to see beside him a little girl with
satined skin and a white dove perched on
her garlands of rose-colored hair. She was
sipping a root beer float in a state of bliss.
He heard the fizz of soda and cream,
smelled the caramel dark; her hair was
waves of petals, her hands were carved
ivory amulets, tiny enough that he could
have worn them around his neck. He said
a prayer to a God he had ceased to believe
in. He vowed to wait for her, to never let
himself love anyone else. But one day she
was not at the counter sipping her float.
She and the enchantment were gone from
the hotel.

Years later the artist who called himself Caliban had an art opening in a

gallery. The paintings were of monsters from the depths of hell, monsters with gaping mouths and huge bleeding hands. Sometimes Caliban set real bones and skulls into the thick smeary dark paint. Once he put an entire skeleton in. He called the skeleton Mister Bones. The paintings were huge and sold for lots of money but Caliban was miserable. He vowed he would start painting something beautiful. The trouble was, he never saw anything that he believed was truly beautiful. Until that night.

She was standing among the monsters and casting an eerie light onto the bleak canvases. In that light the monsters appeared to be transforming. They seemed to be getting smaller and weaker. Their mouths closed and their hands dropped sheepishly to their sides. No one wanted to purchase these watered-down versions of Caliban's earlier work. They left the gallery in droves until the only person left was a woman who resembled Nefertiti with blushing hair. Caliban approached her and said, "What have you done to the monsters?" The woman smiled and it was like a temple full of candles, like a garden full of white flowers, like the spread of wings. At that moment Caliban knew that she was the little girl at the soda fountain in the jade-green hotel and that from then on he would never paint or love anyone else.

Thorn

I lay on the bed in the dark, touching the bone basket of my ribs, the bone bird of my hips. Although I was wrapped in blankets I felt cold. The room I shared with Thorn was really a sunporch. All summer we had looked out at the fruit-heavy plum tree and the honeysuckle vines and felt the sun through the glass panes. But now it was autumn, and raining. The tree in the yard reminded me of Mister Bones.

My stomach made noises like a cat as I curled up under the blankets. I did not shut my eyes. I did not want to see what was there in my head—the naked body, all bones and whiteness, crouched in a marble box. I could not escape the voice that easily.

I will not eat cakes or cookies or food. I will be thin, thin, pure. I will be pure and empty. Weight dropping off. Ninety-nine . . . ninety-five . . . ninety-two . . . ninety. Just one more to eighty-nine. Where does it go? Where in the universe does it go?

That morning I had walked all the way to campus, across campus, up into the hills of Northside to the hospital, knowing it would burn off the apple I had eaten when I woke up. On the way I passed a group of homeless men and women spare-changing near People's Park. Among them was a beautiful young blond girl in tight jeans. She whirled around and her face was not a girl's at all—a toothless crone's collapsing into itself.

The psychiatrist asked, "Why are you starving yourself?" and I had known all the right answers. Escaping the responsibilities of growing up; having control over something at least; being beautiful, perfect like my mother, making my father love me. I smiled secretly to myself that I could know all this and still skip dinner, still jog five miles in the rain. I did not tell the psychiatrist about Thorn.

During the first months away from home I had wandered on the campus looking into the faces of the men, searching.

They were sleeping on Shakespeare in the
cathedral-like library, slurping coffee from
huge cut-glass goblets at cafes; they were
on running shoes, on wheels. None of
them was the one I was looking for. Then
at a party in a warehouse near the Oakland
border, I had seen Thorn wearing a white
cotton shirt and drinking gin. There was
something about him that reminded me
of my father when he was young. Thorn
was doing magic tricks, making people's
jewelry vanish. He pulled a tiny orange
paper parasol from behind my ear and
walked me to the dorm. The air smelled
rich and sooty after the rain, like flowers
could grow in it.

"You look like a poet," I said, when he
told me what was in the notebook with the
torn binding.

"It's all just this pretentious self-centered angst."

I said I bet it wasn't.

He said, "Besides, don't I look more like a magician?"

When he kissed me good-night and held me for a moment I was surprised at how cool his skin felt, except for the heat in the hollow of his back. The memory of that heat stayed in my palms all night. When I touched myself in my dorm bed, I said his name out loud in the dark. I wanted to tell him that maybe he had already changed something.

A few nights later we went to a cafe in the city with sawdust floors and steamy windows. Thorn lit my cigarette and talked about the beats who used to hang out there, bopping berets, snapping fingers, guzzling wine.

A skinhead with a swastika tattoo
walked by the window screaming and I felt
my knuckles whiten around the edge of the
table.

"I don't think violence is ever justi-
fied," Thorn said, pouring me more bright
gold from the glass decanter.

I wanted to make the swastika bleed.
But to Thorn I just said, "Never?"

He must have heard the tightness in my
voice. He looked out across Broadway at
the nipples of a neon sex goddess flashing
on and off. "I know. Maybe."

He bit his lip. It was soft in contrast to
his narrow aristocratic-looking face. I felt
my thighs weaken, like the muscles were
sponges soaking up wine.

That night in his tiny dorm bed, the
heat I had discovered in his back pulsed

through my whole body. I looked into his eyes and saw myself trapped in the irises.

After that, we were inseparable, always holding hands, always touching, bound together. Nothing else, no one else mattered. It was easier that way. Most weekends we took the BART to the city and pretended to be different people.

"What do you think of the way Vermeer used light?" I asked him. We were on the lawn beside the ornate terracotta dome, watching the swans and ducks gliding on the pool. I was playing the older woman, the artist with a gingerbread house full of charcoal drawings and flowering cactus plants that you had to water very gently by pouring drops just into the center of the spiny leaves. The frankincense and myrrh woman with the huge hoop earrings and turquoise rings from a New Mexican reservation and the lines carved around her eyes.

He squinted up at the straining muscular backs of the stone men supporting the dome. "You'll have to take me to some museums," he said. He was being the young man on the road, following the sun because gray weather made him suicidal, writing his poetry in his mind in diners and gas station men's rooms across the country. "But I did see a show of Hopper once. And I like his light. It was kind of lonely or something."

Or, "'The world's a mess, it's in my kiss,' like John and Exene say," he mumbled. We were in a leather store on Market Street being punks on acid with skunk-striped hair and steel-toed boots.

"Fuck yes. Let's go to Mexico, shave our heads, get drugs, wear beads and silver."

Once, alone on the train, late at night, he pretended to be a professor teaching me about Dickinson.

"Why do you think she loved death so much?"

"She loved life."

"But she wrote about riding in his carriage, sleeping with him."

"That's because she loved life too much," I said.

He reached up behind me, so quiet, and slipped his hands inside my shirt.

If Death is your father, you don't ever have to worry about what part of his body the disease will strike next. If Death is your lover, you don't have to be afraid that he will ever leave you.

We were opium-den dragon chasers in Chinatown, Santeria priests in the Mission,

gay men in the Castro, tie-dyed acidhead
sandalwood-scented runaways on Haight
Street. No matter what roles we played at
the end of the night we merged in the bed.
We even began to look alike.

"If I were a boy I'd be you."

"You'd be wilder."

I chopped my hair shorter again and
wore his shirts. The shirts smelled musky,
like sweat and like peppermint soap, like
him or like us, I wasn't sure. Sometimes I
put eyeliner on him and he was prettier than
I was. Men in the Castro stared. Leather-
chapped chaps and pale pierced boys.

Then I gained a few pounds from all
the Sunday croissants that soaked buttery
stains through the napkins, the Kahlua and
milks, and from the birth control pills I had
started to take. I dug my nails into unfa-

miliar flesh—the breasts, the hips. It was like they belonged to another girl. Thorn stayed so thin.

Once, near the end of the semester, I broke an empty gin bottle—threw it to the floor and felt it shatter as if it were a part of me, as if the bones in my wrist were glass splintering. Thorn held me, hunching his shoulders to shield me, and I choked on my tears, squeezing my belly, disgusted by the extra pounds that had lumped themselves there.

In June, Thorn and I moved into the blue wood-frame house full of students. We had to step over two sleeping bodies to get to our glass room. Through the walls we heard moans of love and people screaming at each other. The kitchen floor was always sticky and the refrigerator overflowed with fattening foods; I had dreams of chocolate cakes ascending the stairs and smothering me in my sleep.

But the room was pure, it was cool, it was glass. We filled it with the thin, hard things we had collected—old Iggy Pop and Velvet Underground albums, narrow volumes of Emily Dickinson's poetry, posters of Picasso's blue, bony, ravaged, absinthe-poisoned saltimbanques, a wine bottle holding dried flowers. The room smelled of new paint and the sweet straw mat on the floor.

I went off the pill and started to lose weight. While Thorn was at work at a cafe I lay in the garden sun, letting the warmth burn into me. I waited for Thorn to come home; there was no one else I thought of spending time with. On weekends we took drives along the coast, jogged in the hills, went to museums and flea markets where I bought deteriorating silk slip dresses from the forties. We read poetry in cafes, took photographs of each other. There was a slowness about us. We didn't stay up late anymore, sawdust whispers over wine, beat-love poetry all night.

By the end of the summer something was changing. Thorn seemed preoccupied, distant, staring into his coffee or his book. After we made love we slept apart. The single futon seemed too small for the first time. I would turn away and fill my lungs with air. Thorn ground his teeth in his sleep.

When we went out I noticed all the women—wishing I was tall like that, golden like that. African women rippling beads, braids, sarongs and silver; shiny Asian girls with colty legs; women with flows of

fruit-colored hair; there were broad cheekbones, tiny sculpted noses, gemstone eyes.
A parade of the pieces of women. My
own eyes that were not gemstones, were
not tourmaline or jade or sapphire, darted
from the women to Thorn. I thought of
my mother who was more beautiful than
all of them.

I hadn't gotten my period for two
months so I went to the doctor.

"You're not pregnant," the doctor said,
and I didn't feel relieved or sad, just emp-
tier. "Have you been eating?"

I told Thorn that night, "I think I'm
sick."

He didn't say anything, just looked at
me, glazed. I wanted him to call me darling. Tell me it would be okay. We'll take
care of it. It was what my father might

have said when I was a little girl. I wanted
Thorn to take me out for dinner and order
brown rice and vegetables and white wine.

That night we lay in the darkness in
the bed and I shivered, my stomach
growled.

"Thorn?"

He sighed. "What's wrong?"

"I can't sleep. I feel weak."

"You should eat something then."

He turned over. His back was a fortress
of bone. I curled up, my head under the
covers, wondering what it was I wanted
from him.

I heard the grind of molars next to me
in the bed.

Thorn was hesitating outside of our
door. I heard him rustling. Then he came

in and flicked on the light. It burned my
eyes like a chemical. The rain had darkened his hair, pressed it against his skull.
He held up his empty hands, then reached
behind and brought out a bouquet of roses.

I hated the roses. I couldn't help it. I
hated the pink wet trick roses he was holding. They reminded me of the morning I
woke up to a bed covered in roses he had
stolen from the neighborhood and then
clipped to remove the thorns. The way we
had made love, crushing petals until the
whole steamed-glass room smelled of pollen
and sex. They reminded me of his wounded-
looking mouth as he read his poems.

Thorn handed me the roses and took
off his tweed jacket. The water had gone
through to his shirt so that it stuck to
his thin shoulders and chest. He was

the same white as his shirt.

"Thank you, Thorn," I said in a voice that sounded too controlled, too cold. I didn't mean it to. I put the roses down beside me, trying to keep in mind exactly what I was going to tell him.

"I have to talk to you," I said.

Thorn sat on the narrow bed with me. I could smell the rain that had soaked into him, starring his eyelashes. I tried not to think of how I kissed those eyelids, how the eyelids trembled when he came.

"I'm going home. I dropped out of school today. My parents are coming to get me tomorrow. I'm sorry I didn't tell you first but I have to get out of here. It's not you. I need to be home now."

I had not told the psychiatrist about Thorn. Or about my father.

Nothing my mother could do had helped. Nothing the doctors could do. They had treated him and now there was more.

I had tried not to let my father know about the cat in my stomach, the way my skin bruised at a touch, the metallic ache of my teeth. How the only thing that made me feel calm was seeing the scale register less and less weight. I didn't say that all I wanted was to move back home. Maybe I could help my mother take care of him. If he let me take care of him it might be as if he were taking care of me.

It came out that night on the phone. I started crying to my mother and he took the phone away and made me tell him. The psychiatrist. The lost pounds. The cat, the bones, the metal, the box. And then I heard him speak, in a voice I had almost forgotten.

He said, "Stop saying you're sorry, darling."

He had not called me that in years. He was going to get in the car, even though it hurt him to sit for too long, I knew that, and drive up to bring me home. He had waited until I stopped crying, stopped apologizing, and said, "There's only one condition. We're going to stop for a Foster's Freeze on the way. And you know how I hate eating dessert alone."

I wondered what had happened. Had someone flown down and whispered something into his ear?

One weekend soon after we'd met,
Thorn and I had gone to stay in the house
where he had grown up. Thorn's father
was away on business. The house was an
old wood-and-stone two story with a plot of
wildflowers in front.

"My mother used to call it the
meadow," Thorn said.

Inside the house was icy cold—so that
our breath hung on the air—and dusty.
"My dad's not a great housekeeper,"
Thorn said. We built a fire in the shivery
living room and ate our pasta in front of it.
Then we climbed the creaking cold stairs
to the bedroom with watercolors of wildflowers on the walls, where Thorn's
parents used to sleep, and where no one
slept now.

"He stays downstairs in my room."

I started crying while Thorn was still inside me. I had wanted to ask him if he could feel the crying in himself, then.

"My dad has cancer." It was the first time I'd said it out loud.

And he had just held me, not saying anything, until I fell asleep.

The next night I danced for him in his father's house, removing my clothes, in spite of the cold. I wanted to give him something. I wanted to feel what he felt. I saw his mother, with bright eyes and dusky brown hair and full rosy cheeks, picking flowers from the meadow, painting them in watercolor, reading to her son, listening to him recite his poems. I saw his mother in a hospital bed, bones poking against her skin, while he tried to make her forget with silver rings and vanishing eggs.

After the dance, Thorn cried. And after that, neither of us spoke about my father or Thorn's mother.

Thorn bit his lower lip and turned his head away. He made a soft, nervous sound, almost like a laugh.

"Well, how do you feel? You never say anything anymore."

He breathed hard through his nose. His shoulders heaved. It was as if I could see the feelings locked between his scapulae and in his sternum. He looked at me, narrowing his eyes, breathing hard.

"I love you. I just have to leave. I'm a mess. And my dad is really sick." I was almost screaming. "Can't you say anything?"

"Just . . . let . . . me." He sounded strangled. There was a long silence of rain and breath. I started to sob into my hands. He watched the sobs shake my torso. My body felt like a child's, as small as when I was a child. The roses were lying next to me on the bed. Some of the rainwater had soaked into the quilt.

He did not turn around but stood facing the door, his hands forming fists, his shoulders stooped and rigid. I wanted him to hold me, to take care of me, to make the pain dissolve away. I knew that this wanting was part of what had ruined everything but I wanted it once more anyway. I rubbed my hands along the backs of my thighs to warm them. Then I crossed my arms on my chest and grasped my shoulders. They felt like the skulls of birds.

Finally, Thorn turned. I reached up and he took my hands, warming them in his own. Then he knelt and pressed my hands under his armpits. The heat of his body made my hands ache, then tingle.

We did not make love. We had not made love for at least a month. We had hardly touched for a week. But that night we slept close again, Thorn's hands solid heat on my abdomen.

I dreamed of my body all light and shadows in yards of sheer white lace. I was standing beside Thorn at the end of a corridor and he turned to me, lifting the veil that hid my face. He leaned to kiss me. I parted red lips of a skull revealing fanglike teeth.

"Mister Bones," I said, "pray tell, sir, which one of us is you?"

The next morning Thorn kissed my
eyes. He made a small plastic dove ring
appear out of thin air, unfurled my finger
and slid it on. Then he left.

I lay on the bed waiting for my parents
to come for me.

Smoke

When, at three, he first saw *The Wizard of Oz* on TV, JJ fell in love with Glinda, the good witch. The tulle-haired, glitter-frosted queen with the little people hidden in her frothy cakelike skirt. For years, on every birthday cake he wished that he could find her.

Then, all he wished for was that his mother would get better.

His mother was pale fragrance and paper hands and then she was drowning among bouquets in the metallic hospital. When she died, he wondered what he had done.

His father the TV producer immediately began to collect starlets around the breakfast table, around the TV-shaped pool. They petted JJ with their sharp red-lacquered nails and asked him where he had gotten those beautiful eyes.

They're hers, he wanted to say. And she is watching you. And she wants you to leave.

When he was thirteen, he felt as if he had poison in him. His skin broke out red and sore. He wore a cotton hat slouched over his eyes and got high in his room. The starlets ignored him. His father said, "When are you going to get yourself a gorgeous girl?" His sister Elaine bought him

a tiny guitar with cowboy decals on it. JJ
stood in front of his mirror and sang along
with John Lennon and Elvis. He had
Lennon's bone structure and Elvis's lips.
He was thinking about his sister's friend,
Wendy, whom he had seen in the backseat
of the red 1965 Mustang convertible when
Trina dropped Elaine off one night. She
looked just like Glinda with her hair and
her vintage dress covered with glitter stars.
Maybe this was what John knew when he
first saw Yoko, what Presley felt when he
laid eyes upon Priscilla. Wendy was more
lovely to JJ than any of the starlets. Than
any of the star-gazer lilies his mother had
loved. Than any of the stars in the cosmos.
But he hardly ever got to hang around her;
Elaine didn't bring friends home because
of the starlets and he was too shy to ask.

Then, four years later, Elaine started Babylon with Trina, Jeff and Wendy. One night, she asked her brother to come to a rehearsal.

JJ was tiny but his hands and wrists were broad as if he should have kept growing. Marbly arms and narrow hips. Delicate features and the shadowy blue eyes of—what? Wendy thought—wounded, erotic, narcotic . . . the eyes of a beautiful dead woman.

He was what the band needed. His voice seemed to smolder in his chest before it came out his throat.

Smoke, they started to call him.

"The voices make love onstage," a critic said.

Offstage, Smoke came to Wendy's

apartment with the tiled courtyard and the fountain of demonic-looking cherubim. She was in her densely embroidered antique kimono and lace lingerie, writing songs. She rolled joints expertly and they smoked on her bed with the satin curtains closed, the mirrored ball scattering rainbows and Bowie's voice. Then their bodies were the smoke and color and music. Their eyes were always damp with love now, and their flesh was soaked with the scent of fire and roses.

"Did J and Wendy always have the same face?" Elaine asked Jeff. "He's supposed to be *my* brother!"

Jeff, who always looked hungry, was even hungrier now. He just lit another cigarette. He wanted to set the flowers he had bought for Wendy—again, compulsively—afire.

Wendy made Smoke big vegetarian din-
ners and brought him Native American
tobacco that he had to roll himself. "You'll
have less that way," she said.

She felt like his mother sometimes,
making him wear his coat when it was cold
out, making him eat his dinner. He lay
against her breasts with his eyes closed.
She sang to him and he put his fingers
at the hollow of her throat to hear the
purring hum.

"Wendy-Glinda . . . I dreamed all these
people were trying to make this bush grow
and it wouldn't and then you start singing
and these roses start. . . ."

She laughed and put her fingers into
the cool of his hair. "What do you wish
for?" she asked him.

"For us to be stars. For us to tour

Europe and play the coolest clubs. I used to wish for you."

"See," she said. "It works."

He didn't mention his mother.

They dropped acid and saw the same full purple waves peeling back like the petals of a flesh flower. They took mushrooms in the mountains, washing them down with milk, and thought their brains had melted together, burned under the white mushroom moon. The hash made them giddy—he performed for her, doing an uncanny Edith Piaf that made her scream; then they ate chocolates and kissed for hours. They hated speed, which made their nerves ache. Cocaine was okay once in a while, bolting white bulbs of light through them and making them feel as if they sizzled with beauty, but Smoke got feverish sick once and they cut it out.

But it was the opium they dreamed of. "I keep having visions of dripping blue poppy fields," he said. They smoked it on Wendy's birthday and felt floating on, stung with, clouds of powdered sugar.

"Hansel and Gretel tasting all the candy," Smoke said with an ache in his voice.

"We can't do this too often, babe," she whispered later. "We can't be junkies or anything." But he just licked his papers and rolled a cigarette and gazed across the room to where the mannequin stood in her rhinestones and her orange satin Chinese cocktail dress.

They moved into a house downtown with Elaine and Trina who had finally con-summated the love they'd shared since junior high. Jeff and his new girlfriend Suze moved in, too. They were the only white people in the neighborhood. The house was crumbling—pale paint peeling— but it was beautiful with its gingerbread carvings, like an overgrown dollhouse. They cleaned and hung up lace and strings of lights, glitter stars and the drawings they'd made.

In the smoggy violet of summer evenings they sat on the dilapidated porch playing guitar and singing. The children from the neighborhood came and hid behind the posts, peering out with dark eyes, peering at the whiteness—the flash of what looked like diamonds at Wendy's and Suze's throats and wrists and in Smoke's ear, at their bleached hair. But it was the music that brought the children to sit on

the porch or jump rope and finally sing
along in thin voices.

Maybe it was being around all the children that did it, Wendy thought when her
period didn't come.

Being around all the children and that
night in the rain. They had eaten curry and
samosas at a restaurant shaped like a camera with the front window a giant lens. It
was raining when they left. Smoke shel-
tered her with his leather jacket. Because
she was taller, especially in her heels, she
had to bend over to fit under his arm. They
ran along the sidewalk, laughing in the blue
glaze of streetlights while the cars sliced
through the rain.

"I'm so wet," Wendy gulped, shaking
out her hair when they reached the house.

She remembered his voice like warm

honey in his throat. "Are you?" He pulled her hair away from her face and slid his hand between her legs.

"How do you know she'll be a she?" he asked, when she told them she was pregnant with his girl.

"We're daughter-makers."

She had Smoke's eyes and fine features, Wendy's full lips and smooth skin. She was fragile with bluish shadows under her eyes.

"She's the most beautiful thing in the world but she looks like she'll break," Elaine whispered to Trina.

The doctor found something terribly wrong deep in her spine. When Wendy told Smoke, he lit a cigarette and started coughing—a hoarse aching sound that seemed as if it would never end.

Take my soul, take me instead. During the operation he got down on his knees and prayed that he could exchange his life for hers. He had never felt this way—even when his mother died—that he would have given up everything. He would have given up his songs and the way he saw his voice rippling through the bodies of the girls at the gigs, almost as if he were touching them, and he would have given up the lotus festivals of the drugs and the wizardry of kisses, and he would even have given up, he realized, the one he had thought he loved most. *I would give up my life with Wendy for Eden.* His nose was bleeding, flowing in a red torrent that had the force of his fear.

The operation was a success. After it

was over he fell asleep for an entire day and night. When he woke in the fluorescent haze of the hospital waiting room, he wondered, for a moment, if he were still alive. It was only a partial relief. He was always afraid the disease would return.

One night, sitting on the porch lit with votive candles wrapped in saints, he said to Wendy, "I feel like I poison what I touch." Eden started to cry suddenly, as if she had been slapped. Smoke ground the joint into the ashtray and stood up. Wendy could see Eden's hurting in the hunch of his shoulders and in his staring eyes. He left the house.

He moved out to a windowless basement apartment that was hardly big enough for his single futon. His skin looked chalky and his pupils seemed to be disappearing.

The wanting that had been in his eyes and shoulders, in the veins in his arms and in his mouth when Wendy met him, had come back again. But she couldn't do anything about it now. She started to go out with men, mostly tall, dark, husky men who couldn't sing.

Girls wanted Smoke. Maybe they wanted him more; his small size brought out their maternal instincts and, now, so did his sorrow. Eden liked one of the girls right away. Her name was Echo. Eden showed Echo the cast on her wrist; told her how she'd broken it when she fell; made Echo draw a portrait of Sea Shell, the mermaid doll, on the cast. Eden put her lipstick on without a mirror; she put some on Echo. They danced together. This was the reason Smoke noticed her at all. It was as if

Eden's beauty reflected onto her, making her otherwise matte surface glimmer slightly like the little girl's rose-frost lip gloss.

Eden said, "Someday you will love her," and it made Smoke feel as if she had looked into his eyes like crystal balls but he didn't want to believe her; she and Wendy were all that was in his eyes.

One night after a gig Echo asked if she could come home with him. She wasn't beautiful and he didn't love her so it seemed all right at first. They smoked pot and watched some TV. Then Echo put on "When Doves Cry" and started dancing. She was a completely different person when she danced, lush and feral. She took off her shirt and ran her fingers over her breasts. When she looked at him there were tears in her eyes as if she knew the things that had happened to him. His mother. Wendy. Eden. He remembered what Eden had said about her. Echo came over and knelt between his broad knees and he let her kiss him. She smelled powdery and sweet and nice and her eyes were almost as sad as his but when he felt desire startle up in his heart and groin, for the first time in so long, he pulled away.

"I don't want to hurt anyone," he said as if his throat was sore.

And Echo gathered her things and ran barefoot out the door. He knew she was crying. And that he wanted to cry. But how can I take the risk? he told himself. It's not worth it.

Eden was his goddess. He would sacrifice everything for her to stay in the world.

And one night with this girl wasn't even close to everything. Was it?

As Eden grew up, Wendy made her dresses out of sequin netting, painted flowers on her face and brought her to Hollywood parties and nightclubs where people took their pictures for the local alternative paper nightlife column.

Eden smiled like a woman, went up to some of the men, put her hand in theirs. She asked softly to be photographed. She asked, "Have you known me since I was a baby? Was I a pretty baby?" She shivered and shimmered. Her voice was breathless. Her eyes were more and more Smoke's eyes. Waiting eyes.

She told her own versions of fairy tales, about how the prince did not kiss the princess awake but made love to her to bring her back to life, about how the beast never changed into a prince but gave Beauty little beast children who gnawed savagely at her breasts. When they asked how she knew these things she ran off shrieking like a mad cricket. In the morning she woke Wendy's lovers by crouching on their chests—a pretty gargoyle—and insisting that they tell her their dreams in detail. They fell madly in love, bringing her candy necklaces, writing songs about her, painting her picture.

Rumors spread that she was sick. People looked at Wendy differently, said, "How *are* you?" in a different way. "And how is Eden?" Whenever Eden fell, she broke bones in her wrists and ankles. Raphael the mural artist drew on her cast. Candyman the lead singer of Icon lifted her onstage beside him and she danced. She wore a little rhinestone tiara. She was a star already.

Smoke took Eden to the movies once in a while. Especially *Fantasia*, which was her favorite. She made pictures for him and covered him with kisses. The color on her lips was lipstick, smudged and pink as candy. He hardly let anyone touch him now but usually he didn't shrink away from her. They held hands and walked slow uneasy tiptoe steps as if they weren't sure about remaining on the earth, and their blue eyes seemed to look through to something, some garden, something. Eden never said, "Dad," or asked who her father was and Smoke had asked Wendy not to tell her.

"When is Smoke going to move over here?" was all that Eden said.

He was never going to. He was afraid
that if he broke his vow to give up everything for her, that she would leave. Only
those afternoons at the movies; he allowed
himself that. But not Wendy. His Glinda.
Paradise. Sacrifice.

They still had Babylon, though. Their
new manager, Dean, a tall, dark, husky
man with a goatee, had a party at his glass
house in the hills to celebrate their record
contract—champagne, sushi, coke. Wendy
was kissing Dean on the deck. Eden was
running around ripping long green strands
of hair out of Sea Shell's head. The doll reminded Smoke of Echo. She had told him
that her hair was that green once, mermaid
green. He thought of calling her. Instead
he snorted some white powder and threw a
microphone against the glass wall. It was

like the city shattering into all those little green and red and silver lights. Wendy left Eden with Elaine and Trina and she and Jeff drove Smoke to the hospital with his wounded hand wrapped in Wendy's white silk chiffon scarf. Blood had dripped onto Dean's white carpet. Eden squinted at the stain, as if trying to see it as something else—the shape of a heart.

When she got older, Eden performed with Babylon. She was a tiny Wendy singing in a whisper, her wrist in a cast. Wendy knew it was okay when they were all onstage together. They were a family then and they were one person. Eden was Smoke and Wendy and Eden, and she would grow up to be a child-woman holding the secret of their radiance and their music and their wishes and their love in her pale-milky fragile bones. The garden where no one ever gets old. She would grow up healed and healing because their love had made her, Smoke thought.

This was Smoke's only wish now.

Caliban's Gift

When I left my head was buzzing like a staticky TV screen from no sleep, my body from desire. I had seen Smoke's story when I danced. I saw the fairy girl with her eyes just like his. The one who had taken my hand in the club, painted my lips as if she were bestowing a magical charm. I saw him on his knees in the hospital waiting room, blood gushing from his nose. His wish for her. *Take my soul, take me instead.* He loved her so much, enough to give up everything. I couldn't blame him; she was perfect, more perfect for her fragility, for the fact that she seemed about to leave this earth. I wondered for a moment, if I had gotten sick like that, what would my father have done . . . but you can't think that way.

I climbed up the stairs out of Smoke's apartment, ran barefoot over the dewy lawn, my shoes in my hand. I knew not to drop one. This wasn't anything Cinderella. I might never see him again, let alone expect a visit with a glass slipper. The sky was bleached out and the birds were strangely still. I wanted to stop for a bag of burning-sugar donuts, go home, take a bath and stroke myself to sleep.

The ambulance was parked in front of the house. I saw my mother shivering in a coat over her nightgown. She seemed much smaller, like a child who had not grown into the length of her hair. She said to meet her at the hospital and then she climbed in the ambulance and they shut the doors and drove away. The siren sounded weak, not urgent—hopeless.

I followed through the empty streets. There was a faint metallic light at the edge of the sky now. I thought, what if Smoke and I had made love, slept in, gone out for pancakes, walked in the hills, kissed in the wildflowers while the sun came up to bake the petals. I wouldn't have been here for hours.

My father was lying in the hospital bed and my mother was holding his hand, talking to him. His mouth was open and his eyes were closed. I didn't know if he was taking death in through his mouth and shutting out life with his eyes or the other way around. His skin was the wrong color. I wanted to ask him to open his eyes, please see me once. Or forget about me, just look at her one more time, tell her something. I don't even care if you don't say a word to me but tell her you'll wait for her, she shouldn't hurry, she'll be okay here without you. Because I saw how she was looking at him, as if she wanted to follow, and I couldn't let her. That was one thing I knew. Tell her, I thought.

I went into the cold corridor. A young bald man was limping along on a cane. His eyes were blue—too blue, radioactive. He had long eyelashes, starry, as if they were wet. He didn't look at me. I reached into my wallet for my phone card. There

wasn't anyone to call, really. Not Smoke.
Maybe Thorn with his eyelashes like the
bald man's, his magician's bouquet. But
when I dialed his number in Berkeley,
an answering machine came on, with a
woman's voice saying they weren't there,
leave a message. She was every woman
I'd seen when I was with him, every beautiful woman. I saw her lying on a bed full
of roses he'd picked for her. He had
pulled off each prickle; maybe his hands
bled a little when he did it but he'd been
so thorough that she could roll across
them and no scratch would mar her
perfect—peach or gold or was it teak-
colored?—skin. Why did I think I could
call Thorn now? I'd left him, hadn't I? I
had left him.

My mother never left my father's side. Maybe she was silently chanting spells, incantations. Maybe she believed her magic could bring him back. But two days later the doctor told her it was time, there wasn't a chance anymore. She didn't cry. She let me hold her hand as we walked out of the hospital.

I bought some carrot juice and avocado sandwiches from the health food market down the street. I drove my mother to a park and we sat on the sparse grass in the sun and I tried to make her eat. She hadn't eaten since he'd gone into the hospital. She looked almost as thin as I was now. I thought, she looks like my little sister. My tall, beautiful little sister. I wanted her to comfort me but that was what I was supposed to do.

When we got back home I opened all
the windows to air out the rooms. I picked
some flowers from the garden and made
green tea and lit candles. I ran a bath for
my mother and put in lavender salts. My
mother said, "There's something for you.
In his studio."

I thought, what if it's the painting he's
been promising me. Ever since I moved
back from school he'd been saying he was
going to paint me. Maybe he'd been doing
it in secret from sketches he'd made while
I slept. Me in my grandmother Rose's wedding dress. Maybe it was waiting for me,
his good-bye.

My father's studio had been a green-
house once. One big green glass wall
overlooked my mother's terraced flower

beds. The whole room had a soft garden light. It was chilly and smelled of turpentine. There was a canvas on an easel, a palette smeared with dried gobs of paint and some brushes soaking in a glass. My father had just painted the background of the canvas—a celestial blue. I wondered what he had meant to add. Maybe it was finished.

The wooden box was sitting on a table beside a jar of dried roses and some seashells—iridescent abalone, a rippled pink conch, something I didn't recognize that looked like human bone. My name was painted on the box. I held it for a long time. I didn't want to open it. This little box couldn't contain all I needed from him.

But inside were his best paints, some tubes hardly touched. Cadmium yellow, cerulean blue, yellow ochre, alizarin crimson, titanium white, ultra violet. And there were brushes, silky brushes of every size and shape, some so tiny they reminded me of eyelashes. Pale green artists' pencils with freshly sharpened silvery graphite tips. There was a new little palette and a sketchbook of the finest handmade paper.

The only painting in the studio, besides the blue canvas, was the skeleton, mired in thickly smeared oils. I went and stood in front of it. I said, "I wanted him to see me, Mister Bones."

Bones grinned at me. *Maybe Echo is not meant to be seen.*

She is meant to see.

The White Horse

There was a fire somewhere. First, the charred smell. Then the pieces of ash like peeled flesh. The wind blew them up against the windshield. Gray smoke from under the bridge. She wondered if the house were on fire. When she got off the freeway—home—she would run into his bedroom and let the flames seal it up.

"As a people we had to choose faith over anguish," he had told her. "Otherwise we would all have perished from grief when

it happened. But I had no faith until you."
He was lying in bed, wearing the silk cap
she had made him, his hair mostly gone
from the treatments. "We will always have
each other, Eva."

Now there is nothing, she thought.
She who had always had faith in everything. Trees feathers babies rivers iris
light. Now there was only the torn ash in
the air. Cars all hot chrome burning on the
freeway and the smoke coming up from
underneath. Nothing to go home to except
the canned soups and crackers she had
started eating, the bottles of gin. Days of
pulling things out of closets, putting them
in piles, putting them back. The hours it
took to do the dishes, boiling them clean
of fear. He was wrong about them always
having each other. He was gone. Maybe

she would go home to find the house had burned down.

But it had not burned. Mister Bones was hanging above the fireplace. She made herself shower and put on a black dress her daughter had left behind when she moved out. The party was at Natalie and Stephan's. They had been his colleagues at the university and she recognized most of the people from the few functions she had attended. He never cared much for going out, always preferred to be home alone with her.

"Eva, you look beautiful." Natalie handed her a cocktail. "As always."

She knew this wasn't true. Not that it had been something she'd ever worried about but she knew how much she'd changed, almost overnight. And yet,

Natalie seemed serious. Maybe the starved and charred look of her mourning was considered fashionable. She thought she looked like an Auschwitz survivor. Both she and her daughter living out his past this way.

She took the last sip of alcohol, feeling the burn that she had always hated before.

"I'll go get you another." Natalie ran off and she stood alone, her hands like ice from the glass.

There was a man watching her. She was used to men's eyes but there had always been her husband's love like a screen surrounding her. This man's flesh, stretched taut over high cheekbones and angular chin, was the color of something she had seen today—yes, the ash blown on the freeway. His eyes were light, mesmerizing.

"I've seen you before," he said.

No, she would have remembered his pallor, his bones, his strange light eyes. "I don't think so."

"I know." The man's lips slipped over his teeth. "It looks like you need a drink. May I?"

She shook her head but he took her hand anyway. His palm felt frosty even against her own chill. The veins in his arms had a thorny blue glow. He led her to the bar and grabbed a bottle of gin, pouring it, straight, into a paper cup. It flared electric in her head and he was watching her. His eyes were like full-blown poppies, like sleep.

"It was at a gallery opening. I was a student of his."

She felt herself pulled toward him, falling.

"Come home with me, Eva." His voice cracked tenderly. "If you want. I'll just hold you if you want."

"Yes," she found herself whispering.

His room smelled of the burning, the smoke that had filled her on the freeway. Burnt hair, scented candles and tobacco.

On the walls were black-and-white drawings of emaciated, hairless men and women with sunken eyes. She went over to the bookcase and took out a heavy volume, opened it to some black-and-white photographs of heaps of bones. She looked back at the shelves, dizzy. All the books were about the same subject.

"It's my specialty," he said. "I have studied it since I was a child. That's how I met him. I especially admired his early work. I knew that was his influence even before I read about his life."

She was shivering now.

"Before he met you. It is so fascinating, don't you think? Do you know what the word means? Well, of course you must, Eva. The wife of the expert."

A sacrifice consumed by fire.

"It sounds like it refers to some kind of natural disaster. Or unnatural. Holocaust. But it is a sacrifice. They were sacrificed. For what do you think? Fascinating."

The sudden sound of wings, but a sound like flesh on flesh, not feathers brushing, startled her. A black bird was perched on a metal stand above the bed. The terror of birds she had felt ever since the illness bit at her intestines. She had always loved birds before—they had come

to her, to ornament her and sing her songs
and eat from her hand. But there had been
ravens in the bushes around the hospital.
A pigeon trapped in the house, shudder-
ing against the glass again and again.
Dreams of vicious birds with hooves and
teeth.

The man took her, caught her lips like
slices of meat. He burned like ice cubes. A
searing jolt of numbness. A slick ointment.
She wanted his poison. A sleep without
dreams. The bird's throat made a savage
sound.

"Why would he want to be cremated
after what happened to his people?"
she heard the voice say. "He abandoned
his religion for you. You became his
religion."

When she woke the man was asleep beside her. Her eyes ached dry and her mouth was sore and cracked at the corners. She stood up, her head and stomach swerving with nausea. Slowly she walked to her car. An animal lay in the road, flattened and bloodless as the thing that was supposed to be beating in her chest.

When she got back to the house, the light was whitish lavender and a bird was singing. She stood in the garden that was only weeds now. One veiny iris bloomed in the tangle. Once he had said, "Flowers are reincarnation. They come out of the earth of our ashes. Nothing else looks so soullike." She had worked in this garden for hours to give him the souls to paint.

The garden of weed and he was not there. A disappearance. He was away.

That was all. How else to explain?

There were no flowers anymore. But the iris had appeared overnight. She knelt in the earth before it. "They come out of the earth of our ashes," the flower whispered.

She pressed her lips to its round head and felt it tremble. She fit her whole mouth around and it seemed to stiffen with excitement.

When she looked up the white horse was standing there as if the fog had taken this shape. His muscled moon-silver body. His toss of mane and tail. The long shivery slope of his nose. She moved toward him as slowly as possible, holding her breath. In that dreamtime she didn't question how he could be here; all she knew was that she needed to touch him. She put out her hand

and he hesitated, a tremor passing through both of them, before he reached out and nuzzled her. He was warm and she felt the delicate jets of the breath through tremulous nostrils, the bristling hairs, the hard strength of teeth beneath the furl of his lip. His eyes were what made her know. The big dark brown tender light-filled orbs that were the eyes of her husband.

Psycho pomp. Spirit guide.

She remembered standing on the cliff with her daughter, scattering the ashes over the sea. When they got home she said, "I'm not sure I can go on without him." She hadn't meant to say it. Echo had grabbed her shoulders. "No, I need you." Her girl, her best flower, her sad mermaid. Remember when her hair was green at seventeen? Remember twelve dancing through the house like a force of nature? Cascading flood raging fire. Remember eight when she made the valentine with the antique lace doily and the tiny round mirrors—remnants from a skirt from India—and the pressed flowers? For the most wonderful mother in the world. You are our angel. No, baby, not an angel. "You can't leave, Mom." She had wanted to stay and help her daughter, give her love to the one who was living but she was so tired without him.

And why had he chosen this? Ashes. So she had become ashes with nothing left inside of her. No gardens feasts healing love. Her mind empty. Except for some dim thoughts of needing to sleep.

Now she did not want to sleep. She would call Echo. She would feed her.

Wasn't Echo too thin still? Too pale. Was
she smoking cigarettes? Eva thought she'd
smelled them in her daughter's hair. What
was Echo feeling? Did she know how much
her father had loved her? Maybe she was
afraid to know, just as he had been afraid
to show her. He was gone now. Would it
make it only hurt her more? Would she
hear it if her mother told her? And was it
true, or something Eva wished were true?
But they would talk. Echo always knew
so much about everyone else. Maybe she
would come and dance, see inside Eva
the way she had seen when she was in the
womb, all-knowing. Maybe she would see
the story of the man with the black bird,
the appearance of the white horse.

Eva and Echo would light candles on
the Sabbath as Eva's mother had done

when she was a child, with the white lace
on her head, saying the blessings. She
wanted to sink herself wrist-deep into the
soil to prepare for flowers. Every day her
tears would water the lawn. The horse
would stay at her side, nuzzling her neck,
nibbling food from her palm, gazing into
her eyes. She would ride him through the
hills at twilight. She would scrub her skin
and rinse out her mouth until Death's
stinging numbing ointment was gone. She
would take down the painting of Mister
Bones.

And the lawn would not burn, the
house would not burn—no, she would not
go back to the man.

Skye

After my father died I started to paint again. He had taught me how to stretch the canvas and prepare it with gesso, how to make an eye alive with a dab of white, lips ready to part with a gleam and a shadow. I wanted him to know I hadn't forgotten. I used the paints he had left me. I made faces, one after another—of the girls. But always with something a little off. Bella's eyes have bars shadowing them, Linda bites her hand, Jolie's mouth bleeds.

It wasn't enough. I wanted to be her—
Beauty. Maybe that was why things
happened the way they did.

I was working at Iris, the gallery where
my father used to show his paintings. When
I was little, the whole street was lined with
galleries and, on opening nights, so
crowded with collectors, bohemians and
celebrities milling around, drinking white
wine from plastic cups, that traffic was
stalled for hours at a time. Now my father's
gallery was the only one left. It was small
and dimly lit. The only light came from the
remaining paintings of my mother, although
those were quickly disappearing. I sat at a
tiny desk cataloguing and filing papers for
the owner, Iris herself, a petite eighty-year-
old actress who liked to waltz down her

staircase dressed in her finery from half a century ago. She entertained me with monologues from Shakespeare and stories about the gallery's glory days. The gentle horror-movie actors, ballet gods with feet like hooves, and bohemian queens in long velvet scarves who were her favorite clients. I kept telling myself I was going to show Iris my paintings but I never did. She was the only person I spoke to all day. The rickety clack of the manual typewriter echoed through the gallery where my mother had once tamed the monsters in my father's paintings.

At night I went home to my apartment in Los Feliz. My rooms were lit all year with Christmas lights and hung with upside-down bunches of dried roses. I made myself a salad for dinner and drank mineral water with lime. Sometimes I thought of Thorn. He had written me a letter saying he had met someone. They were engaged. He hoped I was all right. I moved the plastic dove ring to a different finger but I didn't take it off.

It was getting harder and harder to paint. I told myself I needed to be around people, move my body, something.

I met Nina first. She taught aerobics classes at the gym and I used to stand next to her, looking at all those mysterious muscles—the arcs of her biceps, her ladderlike abdomen, tight rear end, strong, narrow quads, powerful calves. Everything tanned evenly. I wanted that perfection. Maybe, I thought, you can find it without starvation— with protein and sweat and pain becoming perfectly formed, taut body tissue.

She flirted with everyone, going around

while we did sit-ups asking, "You all right, hon?" in her pleasure-promising voice. One time she patted my bare stomach. "You eating, girl?" she asked. I felt as if she had said she loved me.

And then one time we were alone in the Jacuzzi together. Soft bluish light and the sound of the jets and my body was pulsing in the water. She was brown, beaded with wet, shiny. My father did a series of paintings of my mother in water once. She looked like pearls.

Nina asked me my name. She told me that I was doing really well, really committed.

I felt light-headed from the steam and her eyes on me. "You inspire me," I said.

"I'm glad. I hope I make you feel good," she said. "I just hope you're getting enough calories."

I told her I was working on it. I had already gained some weight. I asked how she got her body that way.

"My boyfriend helps. He's pretty tough on me. He says it's all a sacrifice. I mean anything really beautiful takes sacrifice. L.A. was a desert first and now look at it. And going into space. Mark says the *Challenger* crew were like a gift to knowledge, to understanding the universe.

"But you look like you know something about sacrifice," she said.

She tossed her dark hair and the ends, damp from the water, slapped against her dazzling shoulders as she rose from the steam. There was a bruise on her left hip showing through the tan where the skin was thin. She must have seen me flinch at

that one imperfection because she looked
down at it.

"He's crazy," she said. "A biter."

She laughed, wrapping herself in a
thick, red towel. "See you next class."

The next week in the locker room she
was disarmingly naked again, big breasts
exposed, arms lifted above her head as she
brushed her hair. I was asking her about
the best foods to eat.

"I live on fish and brown rice and vegetables, but a lot of everything. Hardly any
fats, though. There's this great restaurant
in West Hollywood we always go to. Mark
and I'll take you. He knows everything
about that stuff."

I met them in the shady courtyard restaurant where tanned people sat discussing
astrology or reading movie scripts. Nina

wore a short black dress and the muscles in her calves were flexed even more than usual from the tilt of her high-heeled sandals. Her hair was slicked back and her mouth was very red.

"This is Mark."

He was huge, perfectly built, with the kind of skin that looks like the sun is shining from underneath it. His teeth were white, big.

The actor-handsome waiter came with menus and said, "Hi, you guys. I'm surprised you're here when Skye's off."

Nina smiled at him, stroking her shoulders like they were kittens. "I knew you'd give us free soup anyway, Charlie."

When he left, she told me, "Skye's my baby brother. That's with an *e*. He works here and always gets us free stuff. Well . . .

he used to." She and Mark exchanged a
look.

We ordered and the waiter brought carrot juice, miso soup, cold cold salads with
grated vegetables, a basket of corn bread.
Mark watched me while I ate.

"She's really pretty. Don't you think
so, Nina?"

"I told you already," Nina said.

I looked down.

"I mean unusual looking, right? Not
what you'd usually consider attractive but it
works."

"I think you're embarrassing her,"
Nina said.

When his food came, he said, "Fish is
the perfect food." He squeezed a lemon
slice, lifted a pink segment of salmon with
his chopsticks.

"But he eats steak, too," Nina said. "Really bloody. He just doesn't like to admit it."

"Once in a while flesh is great for you." He kept staring at her. "You should train," he said. I realized he was talking to me. "You have a cute little body. You could get to be really amazing. Nina looked like you before she met me. Kind of anorexic."

"We'll help you," Nina said.

They both turned to look at me.

We started the next week. I'd sit in the outer-thigh press machine leaning forward, straining, with Mark kneeling between my legs, my hands on his shoulders. Nina would stand with one hip thrust out, telling me to breathe. Or I'd be on my stomach, curling up my calves to work the hammies as

Mark called them, while they stood on either
side of the machine watching me, touching
my butt sometimes. Then I'd lie on my back
while Mark separated and pushed open my
thighs, helping me to stretch.

"It's important to stay flexible. The
quad muscles can get so strong that if
lightning struck, they could go into spasms
and break the bones."

After training we'd go out to eat or
sometimes to the Venice boardwalk to watch
the bodybuilders and skaters, lick nonfat
frozen yogurt, get our fortunes told, work
on our tans. Not that I ever got brown like
they did. My skin freckled and burned.

I don't know what it was, why I needed
them. Maybe because they made me feel
visible. I didn't question anything. I was
bored with my life, with the gallery, my tiny

apartment, too bored to paint anymore, always tired and ravenous except when Mark and Nina were around.

One night after training we went out for sushi and sake. Mark ordered for us and we tried all different kinds of fish— translucent, firm, glossy pieces on neat beds of rice. Mark and Nina had a contest to see who could handle the most wasabi. They gobbed the pale green stuff into their mouths until their eyes teared. We laughed, sipping the rice wine that seemed to shine in our throats. Nina kept leaning up against me, giggling, her hair getting in my face. I felt her breasts pressing. Mark sat watching us quietly, his fingers wrapped around his sake cup. I saw the veins standing out in his tan neck.

After, we went to a bar in Silverlake and

drank shots of tequila and danced. We were wet from tequila sweats, flinging our bodies around in the spill of lights. Wasted. When we left the bar Nina leaned on me, hot skin and cold red silk. She looked up at the full moon.

"It must have been so mysterious before they went there," she said. "Now it's just dust."

Mark came between us, putting his big hands on our shoulders. I felt the current created by our bodies. The wires buzzed. You could almost see blue electricity racing between telephone poles above us, almost smell it.

"Like everything, baby," he said.

They lived in an apartment building called the Isis. It had lotus-shaped columns in front and a lot of orange trees weighed

down with fruit. Their room was all bed,
dominated by this massive bed that became
more and more beds reflected in the mirrors on the walls. On the walls, where there
weren't mirrors, were photos of parts of
lean tan bodybuilder bodies. It took a while
to figure out what was what—knee or
shoulder, breast or hip. Mark lit candles. It
seemed like a thousand candles. There was
music playing—something that gave me a
thrilled feeling in my throat and at the nape
of my neck.

Nina sat on the bed, took a hand mirror and looked into it, pursing her lips. She
held it up to me.

"What do you see in there?"

Lit by candles I saw myself beautiful.
I touched my hair. My nipples showed
through the silk shirt Nina had lent me.

She had said I needed to start wearing new clothes, all my vintage stuff was ghosts.

Mark came over and sat between us. He took the mirror from me and set it on knees that strained the fabric of his jeans. He emptied the coke onto the mirror, making a perfect razor-sharp line with it, gesturing to me. I bent down and inhaled. It sparked through me like exploding crystals, white fireworks. I looked down at my face resting on Mark's knees. My eyes were candles.

Nina inhaled. She sat up, tossing her hair, blinking. The candlelight shone on her brow bone, her lower lip.

"Tell us a story, Mark," she said. I could hear the breath in her voice.

He was gazing into the mirror at his face and the line of white powder. He leaned over and inhaled.

"A story? You want a story?"

"Tell us. Tell us a story about Echo."

He didn't look away from his face. He touched his hair.

"Once there was a girl who loved a beautiful boy but he wouldn't pay any attention to her. He was in love with this girl he saw in a pool of water. He would sit staring at this girl all day long. The girl who loved him went crazy and died and the boy was turned into a flower. He didn't realize he had been in love with his reflection. The Greeks told that, right, Echo? I think it was really about the blood sacrifices they used to make to the gods. To nature. The boy's too beautiful, dies, becomes a flower. There's blood sacrifice in almost every great culture."

Mark looked up at me, took my face in his hands. Nina came and knelt at my feet. I felt her fingers unbuttoning my shirt. I was reflected in the mirrors. I was reflected in their eyes.

I woke with a hangover in my own bed. They must have brought me home but I couldn't remember. My muscles felt water-logged. I looked at myself in the mirror. Something had changed. My skin glowed the way my mother's always did, my eyes looked lit up and I was shaking. I tried to eat something but my stomach clenched so I drank some hot water with lemon out of a rattling cup and slept all day with the curtains shut.

I wanted Mark and Nina but I didn't want them. I didn't go to the gym and I let my answering machine pick up every time the phone rang. Nina was the only one who called, leaving a message saying she and Mark wanted to take me out again soon. I erased her voice. She called again, saying, "Why aren't you at the gym? Mark says you don't want to lose that muscle tone and get fat. Call me, girlfriend."

I didn't want them but I wanted them. I dreamed of our bodies impossibly tangled under water, writhing in seaweed and tentacles, cut by jagged shells, our blood marbling the water. I dreamed of my toes becoming the roots of a tree, my arms extending, growing leaves, becoming branches, my hair a bouquet of fruit blossoms. I woke up and the sheets were wet with sweat. My muscles felt so heavy I could hardly get up and the cramps in my stomach made it impossible to eat anything except a light vegetable broth. But I thought about food all the time. Muscles and bones and blood pleading: steak, sweet potatoes, buttery corn-on-the-cob, quarts of vanilla-bean ice cream, pizza, pancakes, grilled pink salmon steaks. I remembered Mark eating his salmon that first day, his big chewing teeth, moist lips. I thought of the restaurant. Maybe I'd see them there. I'd better not go, I thought. I didn't want to see them. I wanted them. I'd better not go.

The waiter looked like Nina. But Nina without the tan—a younger, pale Nina with dark circles under the eyes. He moved gracefully among the tables like a deer in a forest. There was something hunted about him. When he came over with the menu he smiled. His eyes crinkled up and he had

deep dimples that looked more like lines
because his face was so lean.

I asked if he was Nina's brother.

The smile disappeared. "Yes," he said.
"I'm a friend of Nina and Mark's."

I noticed how thin the skin was over the
bridge of his nose and the top of his cheekbones, almost translucent, lightly freckled.
Those dark circles under his eyes.

"How did you meet them?" he asked
when he brought my food.

I told him about the gym. For some
reason I kept talking. I told him my dad had
died recently, I had dropped out of school
at Berkeley, was working at an art gallery. I
told him how much better I'd been feeling
since I started working out. At first. Maybe
I was hitting some kind of plateau. . . .

When I finished eating he said, "I'd

really like to see you again, where we could talk."

I wrote my name on a napkin and gave it to him. Before I left he looked right into my eyes. I thought of Nina's and Mark's eyes like mouths ready to eat my breasts and legs. Then Skye's eyes disappeared into twinkling crinkles as he smiled and he shook my hand. He had a warm, dry, firm grip.

"I'll call you," he said.

He called the next night and I lay on my bed as the sky darkened, talking to him. The air smelled of the fires that had been burning out of control, and of flowers—honeysuckle and mock orange. Skye asked me about the gallery. I hadn't talked about art since I dropped out of school. Klimt's lovers, sex suggested under a fall and pattern of gold mosaic. Picasso's Blue and Rose periods. Botticelli angels. The Rodin museum in Paris. My favorite Rodin was the *Danaide*, lying on her side with her hair over her face. You could tell by her sinuous back and her hair that she was weeping. Also, *The Cry*. She had her mouth open; you could hear the scream. She reminded me of a fish woman who had been pulled from her water.

"There's this whole world I want to see. I forget sometimes. I can't breathe here," he said.

"Can you see the moon?" I asked watching it rise outside my window.

"They can't make it stop."

"Stop what?"

"Glowing," he said as if he were speaking in his sleep.

We went out on the third of July. I wore
a cream-colored silk 1920s dress that I had
gotten for a few bucks at a flea market. I
didn't care if it was haunted.

Skye came to the door looking like a
pale Nina. I asked him in while I finished
getting ready and when I came out of the
bathroom he was standing in front of one
of my Beauties.

"Is this yours?"

I nodded. "I haven't done many lately."

"Can I see more?" And I showed him.

He stood and looked at each one for a
long time. Then he looked into my eyes.
"You should start again."

I shrugged. I wanted to get away from
the pictures.

We ate at an old Italian restaurant on

Hollywood Boulevard. Skye took a roll from under white linen, cracked the gold crust, buttered the soft inside, handed it to me over the red candle. My stomach was better. He ordered angel hair pasta for us.

"So you work out with my sister."

I nodded and he was silent, frowning into his plate.

"It helps release tension," I said, like I had to explain. "It makes me feel better about myself."

"You sound like me. I used to work out with them. I was trying to do the acting thing. I started training with them but then I realized how obsessive it was. That was my life. It's cool to work out but those guys are obsessed." He paused. "You have a lot of other reasons to feel good anyway. Like your painting."

"Are you acting now?"

"Not commercially. When it comes to losing a part because your eyes are the wrong color, trying to flirt with everyone to get commercial work you don't want that much anyway . . . it kind of made me sick."

"So what now?"

"I don't know. I'm trying to figure it out. I want to do some theater. I'd like to just live, I guess."

After we'd eaten he got up, took my hand, danced me around in front of the bar while an old man in a red vest played piano. It was late and the restaurant was empty. Skye's hair smelled of smoke, corn bread and leaves.

We drove to Santa Monica in his beat-up pickup and walked in the park on the cliffs overlooking the water. Some homeless people slept in the pale green wood lattice-work gazebo or on the damp grass. A man staggered up to us, asking for change. Skye gave him a few bucks, looking straight into his eyes.

"It blows me away to see how people live in this city," he said, his mouth twisting. "This oasis."

We were quiet for a while, walking. I could smell the ocean and it reminded me of how, once, I had wanted to step off the oasis and find another one beneath that churning surface.

"I get so hungry here," I said. "Do you know what I mean? Not just physically."

"There's not much that's very nourishing."

I thought about my job at the gallery, the gym, my mother riding a white horse through the hills, believing it was my father. And wasn't I just as bad, pretending I had forgotten but still waiting for a boy who would never come? Maybe if I got away from this city for a while. Painted again.

Skye turned to me and I saw him very white and almost fragile-looking in the moonlight.

"I know we don't even really know each other but I just think you should be careful with this thing with my sister and Mark. It really fucked me up. I just think you should think about it."

I asked him what he meant and he shivered, hunching into his denim jacket. "Just be careful, okay?"

We stayed there a long time. People started arriving with the pinkish streaks of light to see the fireworks at dawn. We stood against the railing looking out over the pier as the sky exploded with fire flowers. He put his arm lightly around my shoulders.

When we got back to my apartment my heart was pounding. I asked him in and went to the bathroom to wash my face. In the mirror I saw that my eyes were glazed and circled with shadows and my makeup was smudged. My skin looked blotchy. As I stood there staring at myself, feeling a queasiness in my stomach, there was knock on the half-open door and Skye came in. He stood behind me, reflected in the glass.

"Your paintings are amazing," he said. "You shouldn't need Mark and Nina to make you feel beautiful."

I wanted to dance for him then so he could see me, really see. And so I could see him. My hand went to the buttons of my dress, hesitated; our eyes met again in the mirror.

He reached for my wrist. I turned to him, running my free hand through his soft hair. Then my fingers traveled along the side of his face to his throat. I unbuttoned his shirt collar, feeling the warmth. He pulled away. On the smooth, pale skin of his neck I saw a scar—precise, painful looking, the memory of some deep fruitlike wound. But he had pulled away. Had I really seen it?

"Skye?" I said. I shut my eyes and there was an image of three bodies tangled on a bed. Two men and a woman. Candlelight. Mirrors. Blood flowering the sheets. *There's blood sacrifice in almost every culture.*

He turned and I followed him out of my bathroom to the front door.

"Be careful, Echo," he said. Then he left.

I went back into the bathroom and undressed. I took a bath, tenderly soaping my body. I got into bed, held myself as I fell asleep.

I waited for two weeks, hoping he would call. Then I went by the restaurant during his shift but he wasn't there. I called but they said he'd quit. He wasn't listed in the phone book.

I called Nina.

"Where've you been?" she sounded cold.

"I've just been really tired lately," I said. "I haven't been feeling too well. Nina, I called to ask for your brother's number."

"What?" I could hear her breathing through her nostrils. "Skye? You met him? Don't tell me you're all into Skye."

"Could you just give me his number?" Suddenly I didn't care what she thought.

"Listen, girlfriend, my brother's sick. He has a blood disease. And he's always getting people involved with him and then just cutting them off. Just forget about Skye. You have enough of your own problems."

"He has what?"

"Something's wrong with his blood. They're doing tests. I can't believe you got yourself involved with Skye."

"I need to talk to him, Nina. Where is he?"

"Forget it," she said. "Listen, Mark and I are working out tonight and getting dinner. You should come. You'll feel better." The pleasure voice again. As if I'd been forgiven for now.

"Aren't you worried about him?"

"Skye has his own life, okay? He used to be really close to Mark and me but now we don't talk. He's crazy. I mean, it's sad he's sick but you know just because he's my brother doesn't mean I have to like him."

I hung up.

That night I dreamed about Mark. I was standing naked in front of him wanting to dance for him to see inside him and he wouldn't look at me. He was staring into a mirror and nothing stared back. I woke up shaking. I knew I needed to see Mark and Nina again one more time.

"I heard about this guy who went insane. He got into his orange trees so much he went to the hospital and bought human blood for the soil," Mark said, tearing a segment of orange and putting it into Nina's mouth with his long fingers.

"No way, Mark. Someone made that up because of the name of those kind of oranges."

"It's true."

"I don't believe it. Hospitals don't just sell blood like that."

"Maybe he got it some other way."

"You are sick sometimes, Mark."

I was sitting with Mark and Nina on the lawn above the sea. It was dark after a sunset where the sun hung low in the sky like one of Mark's blood-bred oranges. The moon was rising. Nina caressed her shoulders and Mark turned to her. His teeth were white in the moonlight, big, violent.

"Don't you want to be beautiful, Echo? My little blood orange like Nina."

He leaned toward her. I knew the wound would be as fruitlike as the one on Skye's throat. I tried to scream, but it was like in a dream where nothing comes out.

Nina saw the look in my eyes. She just smiled.

Shivering on the bus that would take me home, I knew I would never see them again. And Skye was gone. In my apartment I took out my paints, my canvas, squeezed some color onto the palette my father had given me. A painting of beauty. Maybe not a woman this time. Maybe a crystal, a light, an explosion of lights, a tree covered with suns. The paint I squeezed out was wet and red like blood but it was only paint. A different sacrifice to a different beauty.

Eden

When she was fifteen Eden decided to have the operation. If she didn't have it, eventually she might not be able to dance, or even walk. There had been some damage to her spine when she'd had the earlier surgery as a little girl and it needed to be corrected now. There was the possibility that something could go wrong and leave her paralyzed but Eden was brave. Her mother had raised her to face anything. When you are that sick as a little child that happens. Either you can face anything. Or nothing. Eden was brave.

Eden was tall, with silvery blond hair to her waist and deep-set silver-blue eyes and silvery veins beneath her silver-white skin. She still had the torso of a child, which she tried to disguise with padded bras that were always a bit big. Her small breasts made her cry sometimes. But no boy cared about their size for they saw her hair, her skin, her long graceful limbs. She had a set of acrylic fingernails applied to make her long delicate hands seem even longer. She painted the nails vermilion. People stared at her on the street and in restaurants and inquired if she were a model. She had a tiny cleft in her chin and a devilish curl to her full lips.

When Eden was eleven her mom

Wendy and her dad Jeff moved to
Colorado. They had a pretty little cottage
by a rushing creek. The air was good for
Eden's delicate lungs. Secretly, at the age
of thirteen, she was able to rationalize her
smoking habit better than if she still lived
in L.A. They had kitties and puppies,
goats, chickens and llamas, an organic vegetable garden. Wendy and Jeff opened a
health food restaurant. Eden went to
school and all the boys worshipped her
from afar. She was planning on returning
to L.A. one day and becoming a singer-
songwriter, a techno Joni Mitchell. She
took singing lessons and piano, wrote song
lyrics. She took ballet classes three times a
week and went dancing with her friends on
weekends. She loved to dance. It reminded
her of being onstage as a little girl, of the

love she felt coming up from the audience and the love shining inside of her, able to express itself through the movements of her limbs. Then Eden found out she had to have the operation if she hoped to dance again.

She talked to her mom's friend Smoke the night before she went into surgery. Eden hadn't seem him in years but he always sent her birthday presents and called occasionally. She flirted with him on the phone.

"Do you have any girlfriends yet?" she always asked and he always said, "No, sweetie." And she'd say, "Are you saving yourself for me?" and he'd scold her for being such a flirt. Then she'd reply, "It's because I'm stuck here in Colorado without any rock stars to keep me company.

When are you coming to visit us?"

She had a picture of herself as a little girl onstage with him. He was so sexy and she could tell he loved her. This night, the night before the operation, he said quickly, like trying to get it over with, "Yes, there's somebody but it's not serious," when she asked about girlfriends and she said, "Who?" trying to sound excited and he said, "You know her but you probably don't remember. She met us when you were little. Her name is Echo."

Eden did remember, of course she did. She had predicted this a long time ago. She remembered how Echo had held her hand and danced with her, drawn the mermaid on her cast. Eden knew she was falling in love with Smoke, like all the girls but maybe more. And then, later, Eden had seen her again at a nightclub, looking much thinner, looking so sad, and Eden had tried to get Smoke to go up to her but he hadn't wanted to. She was happy for him, now, that he'd finally found someone, happy for Echo, too. But by the way he acted after, Eden could tell he wished he hadn't told her.

She held the picture of herself and Smoke against her chest on the wheelchair ride to the operating room. It was the thing she focused on as they put her under—the rose-colored light and the spangled tulle and gauze and his deep spinning blue eyes.

He came as soon as Jeff called him. Eden's lungs had collapsed during the operation.

"Wendy needs you. She just keeps saying your name over and over again," Jeff said, trying not to remember the way he'd felt onstage with Wendy and Smoke, as if he didn't exist. That was years ago and she was his now, he told himself, pregnant with his child. All that mattered was helping her and the baby get through this. And Eden.

So Smoke flew in from Los Angeles where he was living in an apartment in Los Feliz with Echo. Smoke was pretty broke so Echo paid for the ticket. She offered to go with him but he said he needed her to stay and take care of things. He'd call her and let her know. Jeff met him at the airport and they sped to the hospital through the ice. Every crystal on the windshield was daggerlike.

Wendy had spoken to a psychic after Eden's lungs collapsed. The psychic had said, "Everyone you know is taking a little of her pain on themselves. There's a man who needs to come see her. He owes her something from another life. He will take her pain."

"JJ," Wendy said and she went back into the tiny dark hospital room where Eden lay like Sleeping Beauty in red Converse high-tops and a metal halo, struggling to breathe. The picture of her and Smoke was on the wall along with all the recent pictures of her dancing and mugging with her friends. Wearing her baggy clothes and with her hair in cornrows or pigtails or flying loose around her head like feathers. Wendy had put the pictures there to remind the nurses of who was beneath the metal and tubes. Smoke came into that room and he was white as Eden's hospital sheets and he was shaking and his blue eyes were like gas flames. He touched Wendy's hand and she looked up and breathed again for the first time it seemed since this had happened, shallow and rough but a breath. She hadn't left Eden's side the whole time, only to call people and use the restroom. She hadn't eaten or slept. She hadn't let Jeff or anyone else spell her but she let him.

He told her, "It will be all right," and he was so fierce electric blue that she let herself believe him, even with the whiteness of his fear.

He took Eden's cold frail hand and sat beside her in the darkness. She was wearing the cast for her spine with the metal halo around her head. He noticed her long red nails, which had been applied the day before the surgery. He noticed the many piercings—her nose, her ears—but they'd made her remove the jewels. Somehow she'd managed to keep on the tiny pink crystal anklet he'd sent her. It fit and he realized he always thought of a little child when he bought her gifts; her bones were still that small around but long now and she had curving hips and of course that womanly face that she'd always had—even as a baby, startling—though the eyelids hid her eyes and he wished so much he could see them. Even this way she was so beautiful it was like crystals of snow inside of him and then those Converse sneakers—it made him want to fall to his knees and scream for her to come all the way back.

"Do you hear me, Eden?"

He thought he saw her eyelids flutter and he put on the Enya tape he'd brought;

he knew it was her favorite. He stayed at her side for so long he couldn't tell how many days had passed. He mostly just sat, playing the tape again, holding her hand. Then sometimes he would speak of how she would get better, how they would swim with dolphins, dance under stars and how she would wear glass slippers and be wor-shipped on a stage made of moonlight. He drew pictures of her as she lay there and he wrote songs that he sang to her and pages of poetry and even in his grief he was so grateful just to be at her side like this, leaving only to run down to the cafe-teria for coffee when Wendy came. He'd walk through the hospital full of dying children and they would smile sometimes, comforting everyone whose worried faces they saw: *Yes, I'll be all right.* The kids in wheelchairs—bald, missing limbs, with their far-seeing eyes reflecting a light that wasn't the fluorescent hospital because that is what so many sick children learned to do. Maybe out of their deep kindness. Maybe afraid that otherwise everyone would leave. It was what his Eden had done—*see me smile, see me put on lipstick see me dance I am happy you mustn't be so afraid, afraid enough to leave.*

"But I left you, didn't I baby?" he breathed. "I left you thinking it would save us and now look what has happened."

Wendy told him what the psychic had said. Wendy had come to bathe Eden and she and Smoke sat together first for a long time whispering in the darkness.

Beautiful Wendy just a little fuller and a few lines around her eyes but otherwise the same except she was Jeff's now, the way he'd always wanted it, and pregnant with his child, her breasts starting to get the way they had been with Eden.

"I do owe her," Smoke said.

"I shouldn't have told you."

"No. Yes you should."

Later, when he thought about it, he knew what it meant.

"Take me instead," he said to the darkness. "Take me instead of her. Take my soul and put it in this body. Let Eden go back to Echo and live in the pale yellow apartment building lit with Christmas lights all year, hung with upside-down bunches of dried roses and Echo's paintings, and she can stay there and make art and music and love."

Echo was weeping whenever he called

her and she wouldn't say anything; she just
cried and said give them my love and he
told Echo how Eden was but really he was
looking forward to getting off the phone
and going back into the dark disinfected
room with his baby.

It seemed to go on and on, this time
together of dolphins and goddesses and
moonlight and flowers and crystals and
angels and grief and terror and weeping
and then finally Eden opened her eyes
and stared at him—her deep-set silver-blue
eyes and they were full of flirting right away
and his heart clenched with joy and she
whispered, "Smoky," and he said, "Hi,
baby."

Eden told him, struggling to take each
breath, "I was in this tunnel and they were
on one end with their rainbow wings and

you were on the other calling me. They were so beautiful but you are stronger."

He left a week later, the day Eden was released from the hospital. He kept telling himself, she is alive and I am still alive. What do I do now, so that she will still be safe? He went back to Echo. She met him at the airport with her leg in a cast. The day after he left she'd tried to stop her car from rolling into the one behind it at a gas station and her leg was caught. "You were helping take her pain," he said.

When they got home he and Echo made love but all he could think about was Eden. He showed Echo the poems and the drawings and a photograph of the fifteen-year-old beauty whom Echo still remembered as a skinny little child who had taken her hand in a nightclub as if wanting to protect her and could put on lipstick without a mirror, much better than she could with one. Echo was so relieved that Eden was okay but she kept crying, for a different reason now. She had understood from the first night she danced for him that Eden was his daughter and Echo also knew that he had not told her this partly because now it was an easier way to let her go. She wished her own father could have loved her the way Smoke loved Eden, even nearly as much.

Smoke wanted to tell Echo he loved her enough that he had wished for his baby's soul to come live with her forever in his body. Would she have understood? He didn't tell her.

Valentine

The moment I met her, I wanted to be Valentine. I was dancing by myself at a club when I saw her sipping her martini, watching me. I saw her as a little girl sitting at a booth with her dashing father. He was all shadows and light, chiaroscuro, like he'd stepped from a black-and-white movie. She was posing for his friends, learning how to flick her eyelashes and purse her lips around an olive. His perfect little doll until he died from the poison in his liver. That

was when it became important that all the
other men see her.

I stopped dancing. The music throbbed
in my head like too much blood. I looked
over at the red-haired woman with the tiny
cartoon character poised on the edge of
her glass.

Valentine smiled at me.

I'd drive up the canyon road to
Valentine's magenta adobe building under
the Hollywood sign. In the evening the sky
was jewelry colors from the sun and smog
and there was a harsh sweetness singeing
the air. Bougainvillea, camellias, geranium
and hibiscus flamed in the gardens, pinker
and redder in the moments before darkness and the impending wash of chilly neon
that would make them pale.

L.A. is a beautiful prostitute with bougainvillea-blossom-pink lips, hair extensions to her waist, stiletto heels straining the muscles in her calves. Promising opiate dazzle if you pay her enough. And she doesn't just want money.

Valentine and I would sit on her bed smoking gold-tipped cigarettes, watching TV and eating greasy take-out Chinese. If we were going to a club, Valentine would lend me a pair of 1950s rhinestone earrings from the earring tree on her deco dresser. We called it the tree because of the metal pieces sticking out like branches and the earrings like candied fruits. Valentine would do my makeup, choosing the powdery shadows to bring out the gold rings she insisted she saw around my pupils.

"You'll make them crazy," she'd say. "We'll find you a love-boy tonight."

But I always felt almost invisible. Her red hair seemed to fill up the dark clubs like colored smoke. Men turned at the sight of that hair, cat eyes and a perfect body in black lace or blue sequins.

Valentine drank martinis like her father. She told me he had been an animator. He had created a character named Teenie Martini, a miniature girl who appeared on the rim of this guy's glass whenever he drank too much.

"There's no one worth our time here," she'd say, draining her drink, and we'd leave the maraschino-poison-cherry-red vinyl booth and the walls hung with dead movie stars, our pockets stuffed with the crispy fried noodles and fortune cookies

they served. Sometimes we'd go to a fast-
food Mexican place, like I used to do as
a kid, eat burritos in Valentine's smoky
Studebaker Lark with the streetlights
buzzing and glazing everything a greenish-
white. Or the late-night Italian joint where
she would peel the netting off of the red
glass candle and slip it over her bare calf
like a stocking. We'd drop crumpled fortunes on guys' plates on the way out and
laugh; none of them were our love-boys.

Sometimes I wondered if I wanted one
anymore, anyway.

We'd go to Valentine's apartment and
watch horror movies on TV until we fell
asleep. She couldn't sleep without the TV
on. If she fell asleep first I'd look at her
pale face, sometimes still masked with
makeup, her violet lids and heart-shaped

lips, and wish I could be her.

Valentine was obsessed with Mitch Kitteridge from the Bullets. Mitch seemed almost twice as tall as she was. He had slicked-back hair and large hands and large features and chilling eyes that could stun you with a glance. The Bullets played all the clubs and Valentine waited backstage, smoking hard. Then she'd follow Mitch around to a few parties. At dawn they'd go back to Mitch's.

"I don't need the TV on to sleep there," she told me. "He acts so tough and hard and cold and then we're alone, in the morning, he makes me Cream of Wheat. Mitch Kitteridge makes me Cream of Wheat!"

I'd never seen Valentine so happy or so beautiful as when she was with Mitch. She hennaed her hair again and bought fuchsia stilettos. Her skin was transparent and her lips were always a little parted. She looked like Teenie Martini, like a little cartoon character or a doll. One of those old-fashioned bisque ones with green glass eyes. Then Mitch stopped calling.

Valentine and I sat on her bed smoking and she talked and talked.

"I know he'll get over it . . . such a dick . . . oh well. He reminded me of my dad—strong silent type. If my dad was still alive I'd probably deal a hell of a lot better with these assholes."

"I know what you mean," I said.

"But he was so beautiful—that Cleo chick is a real airhead. He could never say I love you, though. He was always talking about other women's bodies. He drank too much. But then I just keep thinking of how he kissed me. And the cereal . . . It's so pathetic what will keep you coming back."

I looked at Valentine, powdery and obsessed, and saw the city was wearing her out. With its killing air and its zombie men and its terrible burning beauty. And wearing me out. Sometimes I thought the only reason I stayed was to find that boy who had rescued me from the ocean; I should have given up years ago.

"You need to get out of here," she said. We were watching *Night of the Living Dead* on TV and eating pot-stickers.

I had told her about Felice, a tall thin woman with big slanted yellow eyes who showed her huge cat sculptures at the Iris gallery. She had a place in the East Village that she wanted to sublet at a very cheap rate with the stipulation that I take care of her thirteen felines.

"Not that I know what I'll do without you."

"Come with me," I said.

But I knew she'd never leave. I think she thought she was Jean Harlow reincarnated as a redhead or something. There were pictures of Jean and Marilyn and James Dean on her wall. Hollywood Baby. Once she'd said, "If I ever committed suicide I'd jump the fuck off the Hollywood sign." She rubbed her bare and glitter-dusted arms and smiled a hazy smile.

I knew she'd never leave and that I'd never be Mitch Kitteridge for her. No matter what I did, I'd never make her feel like Teenie Martini. I could make her cereal but it wasn't the same; she'd never fall asleep in my arms without the TV on.

My mother was working in the garden, the white horse she believed was my father standing above her chewing his carrot, sheltering her from the sun so she didn't need a hat. His eyes were a lot like my father's I had to admit.

She stood up, wiping her hands on her jeans. She had started to wear jeans now, instead of the Indian gauze dresses my father liked, and she had cut her cascading hair short. She was just as beautiful as ever—a light shone out of her that reminded me of the crystals she still kept all over the house to catch the sun. She hugged me and I smelled crushed flowers. I felt like I couldn't breathe.

We went into the house. The air was coated with honey from the beeswax candles.

We began to cook the Sabbath meal. My
mother had started celebrating the holi-
days religiously since the night of the man
and the black bird. On Passover when she
set the wine out for the angel Elijah it disappeared and I know she didn't drink it
herself because I kept my eye on her the
whole time.

We made chicken soup and potato
latkes with applesauce and sour cream. We
made a large green salad and a side dish
of peas, carrots and pearl onions. Chocolate macaroons. My mother had started
eating sugar, which she had never touched
when my father was alive. She even drank
a little wine. She was writing a cookbook
of the recipes, the ones she never used to
write down and she'd already found a
publisher. The book was full of mixed-up

world cuisine—Japanese burritos with fresh seared tuna, sweet rice and wasabi; Greek pasta with olives, tomatoes and feta cheese; Jewish pizza with smoked salmon and cream cheese. She lit the candles at the table and said the blessing. She asked me how I was. I usually didn't tell my mother too many things about my life. I knew she would have worried if she'd known about the vampires and how a fairy almost died. I'd never told her how I'd once almost drowned or about the boy on the beach. But now I wanted to tell her about Felice and the apartment in New York and what Valentine had said and how I had decided to move away.

The white horse shuffled his hooves in his corner and looked at me with his liquid eyes. He was almost translucent in the light

like a ghost. Even if he was my father it was
hard to get used to having him inside. My
mother took my hand.

"It's time for you to leave, isn't it?" she
said.

I nodded. My eyes filled with tears.
Maybe she knew, already, about Skye and
Smoke and Eden and even the angel I'd
once found on the beach. Maybe she was
like me, able to see. I watched her face
above the candles. My whole body hurt as
if it were shrinking. I wanted to be able to
fold back up inside her where I had come
from. I wanted to be my mother. I wanted
to be my red-haired bougainvillea Valentine
in her magenta house, Teenie Martini
perched on her glass. Thorn in his white
cotton shirt doing magic tricks and writing
poetry. I had wanted to be Eden. I think I

had even wanted to be Smoke when I first saw him singing on that stage, when he kissed me and I remembered how he had made the most beautiful child whom he loved more than love, and how my father was gone and I was empty.

Valentine was in love with Mitch Kitteridge from the Bullets. Thorn had married the woman he met after I left; they were expecting their second baby. Smoke had moved to the desert. Boys worshipped Eden and she went out dancing every night. I had even glimpsed someone who looked just like Skye in a black-and-white European film about angels. They were all gone in their way but the only one I didn't know anything about was the boy on the beach.

I let my mother hold me against her breast where it was flowers and light and suffocation. I knew I had to leave.

Valentine drove me to the airport. She gave me a silver heart with wings of flame.

I moved into the tiny room with the thirteen cats and got a job as a waitress serving blue corn tamales and kiwi margaritas at a Caribbean restaurant/gallery decorated with altars of roses and candles and spangled velvet wall hangings. The owner, Rodrigo, was a swarthy man with girlish hips who wore so much of his dead grandmother's jewelry that it was a wonder he could lift his hands. One night he pointed to Valentine's silver heart that I wore on a long ribbon so it swung cool against my breasts when I leaned over to serve my tables.

"Healing your heart?" he asked.

When I asked what he meant he said it was a milagro, a charm to heal the part of the body it represented.

On the days I wasn't working I walked around the city. I walked all the way from the tiny stalls selling jewelry and leather and platform boots, the Indian restaurants and macrobiotic places in the Village, to the palatial designer shops, the sushi and French pastries on the Upper East Side. I never liked to take the subway, even when my legs ached and numbing snow was falling. I walked through the park with its zoo and its tunnels and its pretzel and lemonade vendors and its runners and its angel fountain. I went to the Metropolitan Museum every week and picked a room or two to devour. I remembered when my

parents took me to New York when I was
little. I had been afraid of the subways and
the crowds and the smell of garbage. Then
my father took me to the Metropolitan
Museum. I screamed and cried when he
said it was time to leave. I had wanted to
hide somewhere until it closed and live there
forever. I had wanted to lick the paint on the
Impressionist canvases and play in the
Egyptian temple and sleep in the cool stone
lap of the Buddha. My father had brought
me back every day until we left New York.
He said, "Someday maybe you will have
your work in a museum." Now I knew I
could almost live in the Metropolitan—I
could go every day if I wanted.

On the way home I bought food from
the little Korean market on the corner and
started making elaborate meals without

recipes. Sometimes they were disastrous and other times I called my mother to tell her my ideas for her cookbook. I ate seated on the floor with one candle and the thirteen cats. I spent rainy afternoons in bookstores, finishing whole novels before I knew it. But the best thing in my life were the art lessons. My teacher was a tiny blue-eyed Jewish man from Poland who looked Chinese and had known my father. When my money ran out he let me continue my lessons for free. I came to his loft overlooking the Hudson River. It was filled with ancient icons, a collection of bottles, broken teacups and tall green medicinal-smelling plants. We did some yoga poses together before we began.

"Paint your angels and your demons," he told me.

I painted Los Angeles. As soon as I'd
gone away I remembered the watermelon
sunsets, the fruits that seemed to fall from
the sky, the neon flowers and petals of
neon, the secret stone staircases and jungle
gardens. In my mind the city was glowing.
It was fanning its lights like a peacock. It
was a tattooed diva singing torchy songs
and dancing in the burnished gusts of
Santa Ana winds. Its sheer dresses were
catching fire and its hair was a flood and its
hips were causing earthquakes but how
beautiful she was.

It was a city of vampires and devils
but named for angels and I had met one
there. Sometimes I sent my watercolors to
Valentine.

Valentine stayed in L.A., still working
at a video production company. She went

out at night searching for Mitch Kitteridge.
Sometimes she'd have sex with a guy if
he reminded her of Mitch, or if she was
horny enough. She always made them leave
the TV on so she could sleep. When she
was depressed she went shopping for new
shoes or lipstick. The shoes piled up in
her room. Strappy sandals, stilettos, boots,
pumps. At night it seemed to her as if they
were dancing.

She called me on my birthday. I had
spent it in the museum. Then I had taken
myself to dinner at a Thai restaurant decorated in purple silk where they served rose
petals in the salad, chunks of tofu with
jasmine rice, hunks of sugared ginger, man-
goes in coconut milk. I had bought myself
some new art supplies and I was fondling
them by candlelight when the phone rang.

Her voice was so soft I could barely hear it. My heart felt like the milagro—perfectly shaped silver, a healing charm.

"I'm sorry I didn't write a card. Things have been crazy."

I asked her what was wrong. I knew something was. Usually she would have called and just whispered, "Happy birthday, baby." She sounded tired.

"Everything's peachy except I got fired and they turned off the heat in my apartment, the one month it's cold in L.A., and I'm sitting here wearing three pairs of socks and three sweaters and freezing my ass off."

I asked what she was going to do. If she could stay with someone. I told her it shouldn't be too hard for her to find another job.

"I'm damn qualified but this is the worst season for hiring. I could stay with my mother but there is no way. I can't even really take a shower over there without dealing with her shit.

"This city is a bitch," she said. "You paint all the beauty. All the lights and peacocks or whatever. But now all I see is a bitch. This city is a bitch using people up. I've seen it destroy Jenny and my friend Pebbles and Adam but I thought, not me, you know?"

Jenny had had to be hospitalized because she had almost starved herself to death. She had taken it farther than I had. Valentine insisted it was caused by too many rejections from producers who said she wasn't young or sexy enough. Pebbles had been an amazing clothing designer who used stuffed animals and bones in her creations, the "It Girl" of the scene at seventeen until she got so screwed from drugs that now she was working in a garbage dump. Adam was a great guitar player—mind-blowing, Valentine said—who had ODed a week after his band got their first record contract.

I asked Valentine to come stay with me. I told her again about my art teacher and the food I was learning to make and my walks through the city. How I'd finally stopped smoking. I told her about the shoes I saw in shop windows, glowing like magic talismans. How you always had an excuse to buy shoes here because of how much walking you did, not like in L.A.

She laughed and said she didn't need any excuses for shoes. She said, "Oh thank

you, sweetheart, but I can't. I've got to
work this all out."

I imagined her lying beside me under
the antique wedding dress, her hair tickling
my lips, her scent like all the pink and red
flowers. I wanted to beg her but I didn't
say anything.

Then one night, she called again.

She had just come out of the bathroom
dressed in her peach satin kimono with the
green dragon on it, and her green satin
mules, and her French perfume, and she'd
just had a martini in one of her Teenie glasses
with her dad's little cartoon character in-
scribed on it in gold, and the phone rang.

It was an escort service she had signed
up with one night when she was drunk and
hungry and cold. They told her they had a

customer for her. She was low on shampoo
and soap and toilet paper and toast and
milk. She said she'd go.

The hotel smelled of decay. The hall-
ways were painted puke green.

The man was lying on the bedspread.
She had a phobia about hotel bedspreads—
who knew what went on on them and if
anyone ever washed them. The man said,
"You look like a Valentine." His breath
smelled of stale beer and his gut was hairy
and hanging. She told herself, a nice quick
stash o' cash and then she'd get real work.
She was damn qualified, wasn't she?

I thought of Valentine with her red hair
and thin white coughing chest. Once I'd
seen her slip a black lace cobweb of a top
over that perfect sheen of skin. Dreamed
of kissing her lips, as if that might let me

become who she was.

The part that scared her was that afterwards, the next night, they called her
again. He had requested her.

"It was gross because I was flattered in
a way," she said. "And I went and while he
was doing it he started saying he loved me
and crying. And that was what was really
sick."

"You can come stay with me," I said.
"Please, just come stay here."

"Oh you're sweet but I can't leave," she
whispered. "I've got to work this all out."

And I saw her dressed in her silk dragon
kimono, curled in her purple velvet love
seat in her canyon apartment under the
Hollywood sign. The round mirrors were
all draped in black lace as if someone had
died.

Once upon a time I wanted to be Valentine. Now I wanted to return, put the silver heart around her neck, rescue her, become her angel.

But I knew there were only peacocks outside her window. They would wake her in the morning. Those birds scream.

Wings

$\mathcal{E}$cho went down into the subway. She was no longer afraid of the rushing trains, the sunken tracks, the smell of urine, the dank air. She had spent the night in the Metropolitan Museum.

Echo hid in a stall in the ladies' room until it was quiet. Then she slipped out and wandered around all night. She felt as if she'd been in the secret temple of the gods, meeting mummies and griffins and gargoyles and unicorns and saints who came to life in the darkness.

When the subway doors opened Echo walked out fast and that was when she ran into the man. He took her shoulders in his hands and looked into her face. She thought she knew him. But, then, she had just spent a night with the angels in the Metropolitan Museum of Art and fallen asleep on the train home. She could still be dreaming.

He said her name.

If Death is your lover you don't have to be afraid that he will ever leave you. Echo took Mister Bones' hand and started to walk away. What if this man wasn't real? If he would go away again. It had been too long. She had just, after all these years, started to learn that love was not about one boy on a beach pulling you from the waves.

It wasn't about one person at all. Was it?

"Echo," he said again.

He followed her up the stairs into the light. She did not look back at him until she was on the sidewalk in the wash of golden blue morning before the heavy cloying heat had started to settle. Now, if I look at him, she told herself, now, in the light, it will be real.

She turned and saw his curls, the sun glinting on the lenses of his glasses. She had painted him so many times like this. But now he looked dusty and tired. His back was slightly hunched. He wasn't a boy anymore.

How? Echo asked. She didn't say it out loud.

"A friend of mine met your Valentine. I was on my way to your home just now."

"Valentine?"

Echo thought of the man Valentine had told her about. He had been waiting at the motel. He had just wanted to massage Valentine's back all night. Valentine said to Echo, "I know it sounds crazy but you of all people would understand. His eyes weren't human. I don't know how else to describe it. He smelled like crushed lavender and mint. He took my sleeping pills but I haven't needed them since."

Echo was dizzy. The sun, reflected in his glasses, hid the eyes of the man from the subway. She gripped onto a traffic-light post. Someone's shopping bag hit against her thigh. The man moved closer, as if to shelter her.

"She's much better now." He took off his glasses and wiped away a layer of sweat and grime. He squinted at Echo. She smelled blueberries. She hadn't bought any yet.

This man who had rescued her from the ocean. But what about when she was with Thorn, Skye, Smoke? Even Valentine? What about when her father died? He watched her twist the plastic dove ring on her finger.

It was wrong. I wanted you for myself. But it wasn't time yet.

She was shaking. He walked with her. She was trying not to cry. Maybe they had all been her angels, in a way. Delivering her to the next place. Maybe any love we ever have is an angel in whatever form—a little girl fighting death, a white horse who could have been a father once, a boy on the beach.

Echo stopped at the first market and bought some fruit and muffins. Then she was in front of her apartment building.

Someone had hosed down the pavement and the heat was already making it steam. She smelled blueberries—had she bought blueberries?—and the Pacific Ocean at night. It smelled like her childhood. It was like before anyone left, anyone got sick, anyone died. She looked up at her window and thought she saw her grandmother Rose's wedding dress stir like a ghost.

"Why didn't you come to me before?" she asked him. "Why did it take you so long?"

He bent his head against his chest. He looked as if his back ached. His eyes were pleading. *It wasn't the time yet. Now it's time.*

She reached for him, touched his warm back.

Then she reached up inside his T-shirt and felt them. They tickled her hands.

They were matted, damp with sweat. He looked up at her, looked into her eyes, and nodded.

Echo, on the streets of Manhattan where anything can happen if you believe in it enough. Just like anything can happen in the canyons and underground clubs of Los Angeles if you believe. For magic is belief. Her father had believed in her mother. Her mother believed in the white horse. It had taken Echo this long to believe in Echo and that this man could love her enough.

She tugged gently. The flossy feathers pulled away in her hands like cotton candy, the shabby wings disintegrating, falling from his shoulders, leaving his back bony and naked and so warm in her hands.

In Echo's apartment, Rose's wedding dress was filled with light. It looked alive.

Echo lay on the bed and the man took her in his arms.

Then Storm gave Echo back her tears, the ones she had given him so long ago, gave them back deep into her womb, where they would become a child who would never doubt. Who would know that magic is belief and who would believe.

And here I am poised above with my arms spread flying and there are halos of light spinning out of us and yes this is me becoming holy human and my own self.

ACKNOWLEDGMENTS

I would like to thank the following:

My dear friend and editor, Joanna Cotler, for her brilliant help and insight through the many incarnations of this book

My agents, Lydia Willis and Angela Cheng—with admiration

Jessica Shulsinger, Justin Chanda and Sita White for their valuable assistance

Suza Scalora for her Beauties and Alicia Mikles for her book design

My publicist, Paula Shuster

Ron Loewinsohn for early help with some of the stories that would later become parts of Echo

Meredith Osborne

Paul Monroe

Gilda Block

Chris Schuette

and Jasmine